BLOOD

(Part 1)

Affairs of the Heart Series ~ Hollywood

KEW TOWNSEND

Tremmelle Publishing

HOLLYWOOD, CALIFORNIA

Sign up for NEWSLETTER at www.kewtownsend.com

Affairs of the Heart Series
Hollywood

SURRENDER (Part 2)
LIASION (Part 3)
DECEPTION (Part 4)

Affairs of the Heart Series
London

HEART (Part 1)
TEMPTATION (Part 2)
PROMISES (Part 3)
DEVOTED (Part 4)
BETRAYAL (Part 5)

Sign up for NEWSLETTER

kewtownsend.com

CONTENTS

Cast of Characters

Holly Hill — Paralegal at a prestigious law firm in Beverly Hills, California. She is prepared to set a wedding date with a man she didn't love. She wants real love and found it in London with two powerful and charismatic men — Luka Hunter, and then Kaine Walker.

Luka Hunter — Cable Music Television (CMT) Executive, responsible for the 1989 tour launch of *Hurrikaine in* London, England. He's jaded and believes that women want his money and status. But with Holly, he hopes for a chance to start again and fall in love.

Kaine Walker (His Grace, the Duke of Dunnehill) — Frontman and namesake for the rock band *Hurrikaine*, is a jaded and spoiled recluse since the last world tour in 1984. He's accepted that he'll never find a woman to love the real him. During a Hollywood-type kiss in *Hurrikaine's* latest music video, Kaine finds his future in Holly.

Lady Emily Dunnehill-Jamison — Kaine's sister, wife to Nicky Jamison, founding member and lead guitarist in *Hurrikaine*.

Solange Beauvais — a French private detective, and sophisticated fiancée of Ian Montgomery founding member and *Hurrikaine's* keyboardist.

Sarah (Rah) Cromwell — Kaine Walker's red-haired personal assistant that holds an obsessive attachment to him because she met him before the genesis of *Hurrikaine*.

Chapter One

YOU WERE ON MY MIND

August 1989

Holly Hill's Cottage
West Hollywood, California

The man with the bluest angel-eyes walked up to her, oh so close. Eyes that promised to never leave her. Holly Hill looked at Luka Hunter's perfect face, one of an angel sent to guide her out of the dark and twisted valley of rock 'n' roll.

Holly ran her fingers through a long, wispy lock of Luka's sparkling hair. Then she separated the varied colors of gold, spun into his dazzling hair. It was soft, she barely felt the texture roll between her fingers.

Luka's fresh scented breath caressed her face and then he whispered, "Babe, come to me."

Luka took her into his strong, loving arms and laid her down on the plush bed made for two. He gingerly wrapped his arms around her, waiting for her body to settle into the natural fit of his. His voice sounded warm and familiar, like a sweet, summer breeze. How she loved his deep voice, always a healing salve, his words laced with a strong suggestion of a posh British accent. She'd been lucky to find Luka.

Holly ran a red lacquered fingertip across his full, succulent lips splashed with a hint of rose. She watched his tongue dart out to cross over his bottom lip because she wanted to kiss them again.

"At midnight Babe, I'll make you mine."

Those hot moist lips … lips carrying his promise to make her scream with pleasure.

She watched his eyes to-die-for, the brightest blue eyes she'd ever seen, beautiful eyes that sparkled like the sun reflecting on a prism every time he looked at her.

A new start arrived as she lay with Luka.

Luka Hunter was her future … or so she believed.

Chapter Two

SOMEBODY BRING
ME SOME WATER

The beautiful, golden, California sun surfed the tops of the white, capped waves of the Pacific Ocean. They tired of playing hide-and-seek with black, threatening storm clouds, and settled to remain behind a large black cloud. Holly sighed aloud because the drive along Pacific Coast Highway seemed longer. It started to rain, and Luka stopped for a light lunch when the reporters spotted them.

"Does Kaine Walker have other women?" One fat, balding reported blurted as his chubby legs ran to catch them in the restaurant.

"Did Kaine fuck you then jilt you?" Another well-dressed woman pressed with her foul cappuccino breath.

The hideous questions persisted.

Luka covered her head with his jacket after the enthusiastic paparazzi grabbed at them and held her by the waist as they ran for his new, black Corvette waiting for their get-away in the pouring rain.

Holly wrapped her arms around his abdomen, taking in a slow deep breath. Her ribs hurt badly as she cursed under her breath. She pictured Sarah Cromwell's filthy boot crashing into her torso far down in that dark corridor of hell at Friar Manor in London — four long days ago to be exact.

The cowardly attack by Sarah continued until she'd rolled into a ball. Luka paid an obscene amount to the doctor so the incident wouldn't reach the London tabloids. The good news, he'd confirmed that her ribs weren't broken or cracked, but she ached. She'd saved a few muscle relaxers, and she cursed herself for leaving them on the counter of her kitchen.

"Are you okay Babe?" Luka spoke softly, his soothing voice thick with concern.

Holly glanced over to Luka as he drove his shiny convertible, always handsome, always, except his gorgeous face reflected the fury of Kaine. His swollen eye recently opened. They were quite a pair.

"I'm tired," she muttered with a sigh and laid her hand on his resting on the gearshift. She'd found little sleep the last two days, and she wanted to sink back into her bed and sleep for a month. Perhaps when she awoke, this eternal nightmare will have ended, and none of what happened in London would be true, except for Luka.

She looked at her reflection in the car window watching the falling beads of water from a brief rain shower dripping to nowhere.

She'd found the one, Kaine, and lost him. She looked over to Luka, watching him drive up the curving canyon road to her home in the West Hollywood Hills. Now, he was the one. She shook her head confused.

Luka spoke loudly on the phone — always the executive, she stifled a laugh, picturing him with a phone permanently attached to his ear. But he was a Cable Music Television (CMT) executive first, and apparently an extremely well connected executive. His voice faded into the background arranging to meet within the hour, always somewhere to go and someone to meet.

Holly stood next to the door to her gated yard. Luka came close to her, his red-rimmed eyes screamed for the rest too. She wanted to touch his face swollen around his left eye where the discoloration glowed vividly from Kaine's blow outside the hotel in London. That incident marked the final confrontation between the Testosterone Twins. She wondered how badly beaten Kaine's face looked?

"Look at us Luka," she lamented then released another sigh.

"Look what has happened to us because I betrayed him."

She slipped her arm around his shoulders.

"All rubbish! You forget about that lout, go soak in the tub and rest. Don't expect me tonight because I have too many meetings."

But she needed him too.

Holly wanted to lay with him and sleep peacefully in his arms. That's all, sleep. Her body hurt too much for anything else, her heart too confused for anything more.

Somehow, she needed to convince him to stay and pressed her body into his, wrapped her arms around his neck, and shoved her hips into his. She wrapped her leg around his. But, nothing worked. The moment reminiscent of the times in London, Luka would leave.

"Don't give me those eyes Babe. One of these nights I'll make you scream."

"You promise. But ... I'm not sure that would be the best thing for us."

He kissed her because he feared she would send him away forever. And Luka believed a kiss from him would be hard to forget. He let go of her and headed toward her garden descended the stairs, taking two at a time, his long golden hair swaying from side to side.

Holly ran on pure nerves and became more concerned about the cherry sized knot on her head and the dizzy spells she'd been experiencing since surviving the eye of the *Hurrikaine*.

Holly followed Luka into her cottage. She headed straight for the bathroom to look in the mirror. She evaluated her own swallowed skin tone and the dark circles that bagged under her eyes. The one bruised eye shone a lighter shade of black, but getting better.

She returned to Luka waiting in her cozy kitchen area brewing tea while she made herself comfortable on her bed, fit for two, and all dreams of making love with Luka were forgotten.

Holly looked up at him. His eyes said he understood as he always did.

"I'll call you tomorrow. You have a specialist appointment. When you're better, remember you have a standing appointment with CMT."

"What does CMT want with me? Haven't they extracted their pound of flesh with all the sensational headlines generated by me?"

"You'll fancy this. Remember, I'm here, and you're going to be brilliant."

Luka unzipped her Louis Vuitton suitcases and found the novel from the plane.

"I'm enjoying this vampire book. Rest, I will read to you. I want to see what happens next with the Théâtre des Vampires." Luka sat down on the side of the bed, and his eyes invited her to rest.

She obeyed, and slid up the comforter to stretch out and rested her head on his chest, listening to the words resonate from within his body and the soft beat of his heart until she drifted into a peaceful slumber.

Chapter Three

I STILL DO

Holly gazed longingly at the warm, loving body lying beside her dreaming of the erotic pleasure he'd brought her all night. She wove her fingers through thick locks, separating his long dark hair that lay in clumps on the pillow like an open fan. Her hand gently stroked his hair until she placed it ever so gently on his chest to see if his heartbeat drummed on as a mother would with a newborn baby to confirm he was alive. She looked past him to the gold bar of light streaming down reflecting on his damp hair. How passionately she'd loved him. All night long, continually confessing how deeply she loved him and then how desperately she missed him. Her Precious One filled her with his peaceful words, softly riding his warm, moist breath.

"I love you, My Lady Love, forever."

She took his sweet words into her heart.

"Don't ever leave me again. I thought you did not love me anymore," he explained, his words quivering on his lips.

How ridiculous! That he'd believed for one minute that she could love him with such a deep and abiding love in

London and then be able to flip a switch and forget him. She would be the one replaced because he'd returned to a glamorous life. For her it would be life in Hell because everywhere she went were reminders of him — her one and only love.

Kaine, her forever lover.

He leaned over and pulled her close without opening his eyes. She quickly responded with a kiss pressed to his neck and then on to his ear and over his bearded cheek to rest on his parted lips. How terribly she ached, the pain searing from missing him and luscious memories of his kissable lips, she'd kissed, long, and loving, coaxing his tongue, so soft to dance with hers. And before the desire in her grew too great and the tiny fires exploded around her heart.

Then the damned phone rang.

Holly lay in bed, the room dimly lit, and inhaled deep breaths of his strong couture cologne. She pulled his *Hurrikaine* jacket off the bedpost, pushed her arms into the sleeves, and wrapped the front of her chest. She shook her head, wishing her dream lover hadn't been a creation of her broken heart.

Another ring, another intruder.

Finally, a familiar voice on the answering machine called out to her.

"Holly, are you there?"

She grabbed the cordless phone, stretching tender muscles, recognizing her dear friend's voice.

"I'm here Solange."

Solange Beauvais' French accent was coolly soothing to Holly's frayed nerves.

Solange was Ian Montgomery's fiancée, the keyboard player for *Hurrikaine* and Kaine's best friend. More importantly, Solange befriended her those last dreadful days in London.

"Are you well?"

"As well as can be expected, Solange."

"I saw the news on CMT, Luka, and Kaine, their fight in London," she announced.

"Great! Caught on tape, I bet CMT loved that!"

"Things look hopeless but try to have faith."

"I haven't any strength to have faith in Kaine after betraying him."

"I want you to understand, I don't blame you. Ian and I are sorry about how things turned out. But Kaine loves you."

There was chilly silence.

"Thank you. But please remember Luka. He's been with me most of the time since I last saw you."

"I've heard. It's a tough time, and Luka can be charming. Try to ease off from him if you can. Otherwise, he'll become increasingly intense."

"Luka? Intense? He's been an angel sent to guide me on my path to Hell with Kaine."

"If you say so, doesn't sound like Luka. Oh, I don't understand anything anymore. But I hated leaving you with Luka," she confessed with deep frustration.

Neither did Holly.

But the truth stared her in the face.

Her love affair with Kaine had finished.

Her guilt and embarrassment over her betrayal with Luka on Kaine's special night was too strong to overcome any thoughts of reconciling with Kaine. She simply couldn't face him. The fact that he forgave her and wanted her in Paris to marry him only served to make her shame rattle her to the core. He didn't deserve her, and she'd never face him. The dynamic and always charismatic Kaine Walker was out of her life.

As if to cheer her sagging spirits, Solange promised to pass on progress reports from Ian about Kaine. Holly wasn't sure she wanted to know.

Solange explained. "I have to stay here in San Marin for a while with Ian's family to arrange the wedding and attend a thousand bridal showers. I'll need a break soon. I'm hoping you will fly up and join me, see San Francisco's sights and the opera?"

It sounded intriguing, but Holly wanted to hide at home, lick her wounds and heal.

"Maybe, another time," Holly tried to sound as if promising.

"Of course, how thoughtless of me, another time, of course," Solange apologized, and then became quiet.

The hairs bristle on the back of Holly's neck, wondering what was coming next.

"I'd hoped to ask you in person, to ask a favor of you."

Holly squeezed her eyes shut, praying it had nothing to do with Kaine.

"Would you consent to be one of my bridesmaids? Ian and I would love it if you would join in the celebration and say yes."

Wedding?

Yesterday would have been her wedding day to Kaine in

Paris. Holly sat quietly for a long moment, bridesmaid, and not the bride.

Oh, Kaine how had this happened?

"Yes, Solange, I would be honored," she remarked biting her lip to force the burning tears to stay at bay.

Solange gave her a few details, promised to keep in touch, and said goodbye.

Holly pulled the comforter back up around her chin, cuddled with Kaine's jacket and her memories. She grabbed the remote control to channel surf and stopped on CMT where the news report screamed **HURRIKAINE UPDATE** and ran the headlining story.

There for the entire world to see was the footage of Kaine and Luka in a fistfight in the lobby of Kaine's posh hotel in London.

The broadcaster reported.

"His Grace, Kaine Walker, Duke of Dunnehill, and longtime manager Luka Hunter, 'duke' it out over the weekend. No one close to the band is talking about why Walker and Hunter hold such a physical difference of opinion.

"Speculation is because Hunter decided to leave the *Hurrikaine* organization to come work for yours truly at CMT earlier than expected. While Hunter sustained facial and body injuries, another report from hospital officials in France stated at a press conference yesterday that Walker broke his hand."

A short sound bite followed, and a specialist detailed the extent of Kaine's broken hand, explaining that it would be at least six weeks before he would play the guitar.

Holly hung her head.

Her hair fell forward as her face flooded with guilt.

It was all her fault, and so unnecessary.

The newscaster returned to report.

"No word yet on the whereabouts of the Heart of the *Hurrikaine*, Miss Holly Hill from the famed Collins murder trial defense team. Perhaps she is playing it cool and waiting for the storm to blow over."

Holly threw a pillow at the TV set. Some disgusting attempt at humor at her expense. Well, the storm blew over, and she and Luka survived together — though barely intact.

CMT followed the broadcast with the "One Love" video, her first time seeing *Hurrikaine's* first music video knowing the principal players.

Solange, sweet Solange dressed in black lingerie clearly indicative of the rock genre exploiting women and for a moment, was surprised Solange agreed. Then the camera flashed on Ian and the bright love shining in his eyes told her why. Solange would have done anything for Ian. The camera moved to Kaine, how perfectly darling.

Always. Forever.

The camera swung to Solange once again, and the poses were provocative and compromising, but she was beautiful. Holly couldn't have performed as professional Solange. Her role in the "Now That I've Found You" video was tame by comparison. Luka dressed her in a long, black lace dress at the Hard Rock Café in London — comparatively easy, considering her directions was to stand still and kiss Kaine.

Kaine's memory flowed fresh and painful. She exhaled from the punch in her stomach. And what was she going to do about the ache where her heart once lived?

Hot stinging tears of betrayal swamped her once again. She couldn't take any more memories. Not even the fairy tale ones of the video shoot at the castle dressed in the white, gauzy maiden's dress riding on the back of the horse behind Kaine.

No!

The pain unbearable, too great, crippling her, rendering her useless.

She moved to take hold of the remote and change the channel when her mouth dropped open and then her eyes widened with horror.

She saw the words in the corner of the screen.

EXCLUSIVE
Hurrikaine
NOW THAT I'VE FOUND YOU
Lost Dreams … Lost Illusions Tour
1989 CD single collection
Director: Luka Hunter

The screen filled with darkness and then opened with one white light shining down on her head. She stood locked in the black and white celluloid moment, waiting for Kaine. She jumped out of bed, ripping and stretching groups of sore muscles, but she didn't care.

She popped a video cartridge into the gaping mouth of the VCR and pressed record and watched her first kiss with Kaine with her arms wrapped around him. His impassioned eyes following her every move. Footage of the castle followed and was pure magic.

How had she lost him?

At the end of the video, Holly pressed rewind and then play. She sat back jet lagged, worn-out, sore and beaten, unconscious to the tiny spark of hope growing in the graveyard of her heart.

She wrapped herself in Kaine's jacket, pressed rewind, and played the video again and again and again.

Chapter Four

BAD GIRL

Holly continued to slip deeper into a self-induced seclusion. Food made her throw up, she seldom ate, and she rarely answered the phone. She sat pushing rewind and play, rewind and play.

Holly heard from Solange. All of Ian's family and friends wanted to throw lavish parties and dinners in honor of her impending nuptials. Reports from Ian about Kaine upset her and were always negative. He was heavily into alcohol, unhappy, depressed and generally a bastard.

Brett left a few messages encouraging her to meet him for lunch. Luka called daily to reschedule the CMT meeting and continually tried coaxing her out with star-studded dinner invitations or with her choice of L.A.'s A-list backstage concert venues. She wouldn't even answer her door to him.

Luka wanted to send a private nurse to look in on her every day. Even that had been unacceptable to her. She'd had time to think about how in love with Kaine, she was. And every time she thought of Luka, revulsion and embarrassment clung to her. How could she have thrown herself at Luka to the point where she couldn't face Kaine anymore? The last time she'd seen Luka he'd guarded his feelings. But forgetting Kaine Walker was not as easy as she would have thought it was going to be.

In fact, impossible.

She hated the strained relationship forced between her and Luka. He'd known what would happen if he were caught with her kissing her. It would mean the end of Kaine Walker.

And it was.

Holly wondered how much of this situation he'd planned and was his fault. She didn't want to explain anything to him, too miserable and depressed to explain anything to him. Thankfully, he was too much of a gentleman to push her. He'd left her alone with her scented jacket, hopeless memories, clicking the remote to move the videotape from rewind to play.

Holly briefly spoke with her parents admonishing them for continually throwing Luka in her face, reminding her, how wonderful he was. She understood they meant well. And with only meeting Luka once he had charmed them into wanting him for a son-in-law.

The print and film press perched outside on her curb made it impossible to leave her house. They covered both entrances, and she was tired of being hounded with a barrage of questions about her break up with Kaine. Of course, the fistfight between Luka and Kaine was on the cover of every tabloid threw at her doorway by the press to provoke her. And everyone wanted to know why the Heart of the *Hurrikaine* wasn't with Kaine? Therefore, Holly hid in her private hell of loneliness and sank into a deeper depression, along with her dark shadow thoughts of her blood dripping, spilling down her wrist.

Holly didn't care how many dark weeks passed before one bright and sunny day, Luka appeared at her door unannounced.

"If you don't let me in Holly, I'm going to kick the bloody door down, and you'll see it all on the tabloid shows tonight on the telly."

She reluctantly opened the door.

Luka.

He was carrying bags full of nourishing groceries. She smelled his favorite, Chinese take-out.

She could see it in his eyes as he fought not to let on how appalled he was when he found her cozy place untouched by anyone for weeks. He opened the windows to air the cottage.

She caught a glimpse of her waist length, dark hair in the windowpane, a mix of matte and stringy knots. She didn't remember the last time attention was given to basic hygiene, nor knew what she wore under Kaine's jacket. She looked down to see her bare legs and remnants of red polish on her toes.

Naked.

She didn't care.

Luka rumbled around her kitchen cleaning as he went along, making small talk, she barely heard while Luka arranged the Chinese food in an attractive table setting. His aristocratic upbringing was showing again. He thought of everything. Folded cloth napkins and champagne glasses filled with herbal iced tea, even a fragrant red rosebud in a crystal vase.

She forced a tiny smile. Why did she treat Luka so horribly?

"I'm sorry."

"Babe, I do understand," he assured her as he pulled the letterman jacket from her body.

Holly didn't flinch as his eyes caressed her naked figure.

He leaned over and handed her a crumpled T-shirt he scooped up from the floor as he advised.

"You've had to have time to purge him from your system your way. Nobody could do it for you. But make no mistake. You're a strong lady. Remember that. You will be fine."

Yes, once she'd remained strong. She'd found her strength on the London airport tarmac when she'd decided to let Kaine go to keep him safe. But lately, she acted more stupid and weak.

Luka walked up real close, the scent of him clean, and the scent of her future. His face as handsome as ever had one eye slightly discolored, and a bright red scar followed the line of his cheekbone. She reached out and lightly touched his only imperfection.

"I barely got out within an inch of my life." He smiled and laughed at his joke.

Yes, the cut was about an inch long. But it glowed on his gorgeous face. His lips were healed, smooth, looking soft and perfect. They looked like they needed to be kissed again and again and again. Luka, her beautiful Prince Charming returned for her, and he looked damn good.

Holly leaned into him as if he was all the strength she would ever need. His crisp, white Brooks Bros., shirt welcomed her caress. His soft blue Levi's, inviting as she wrapped her leg around his.

His warm hand slid around her waist, so familiar.

She looked up at him and whispered, "Give me time."

"If that's what you need. We have the gift of time, Babe. You believe you love him." But what he didn't say she saw in his eyes; his bright blue eyes to-die-for — *I love you too.* But was his love strong enough to make her forget?

"Come here Babe. Have a sit. Eat. After, I want you to soak your depression away in a hot bath."

She admitted the Chinese food tasted fantastic and over dinner, he lavished exclusive invitations to see the glamor of Hollywood that had been lost to her for years. She regretfully declined, and he did not push. While she ate, he ran a relaxing vanilla-scented tub and when she walked in ready to sink into the hot healing water she'd found the bathroom scrubbed to a glistening shine. "Do you do windows?" She joked.

"I'd do yours." He gushed and winked.

"Why are you so good to me? I've acted awful, like a spoiled brat. I've put you off these last three weeks since we returned from London, and you come here forgiving me."

"Seems you bring out the best in me," he said.

"Luka? How?"

"This is not a side of me, I'm using to share. But it would seem I trust you, Holly. We trust each other. My leaving *Hurrikaine* wasn't as easy as I made it look. They were my life, my family for all of my adult life. Sure, during the four years between the last tour until today, things changed. But I was in constant contact with the band and then spent the last two years setting up this tour.

"Now? I've left for good, and everything's changed again,

and bigger changes are going on in my life. Then I met you, and everything changed again. I barely know which direction I'm headed in anymore, too many changes, too fast. And you didn't deserve to be treated as you were by Kaine when he found us together. But it happened and, we have to soldier on, Babe. We have to go on day after day creating a new life."

His words wise and his eyes were convincing.

"We can do that together Babe." Luka stopped talking because he had moved closer; he'd bent and kissed her cheek.

She smiled the scent of him heavenly.

"Time will make everything better." He quickly assured.

He took the surface cleaner and paper towels out of the bathroom. She sat in the warm water, letting his sage words sink in when, of course, the phone rang.

"Let it record the message."

"As you wish."

Brett.

Rotten timing.

"Holly I know you're there. I'm tired of calling. It's been three weeks. I'm worried, but if this distance is the way, you want it…."

He expressed with defeat lacing his voice.

"I wanted you to remember I love you."

It was true, he did. But she was numb, other than the growing pain of loneliness for Kaine residing deep in her heart.

Brett added to resolve. "I don't understand what has happened, but I'll wait for you to call."

She heard the hurt and worry in Brett's voice. He'd grown up with her, and she read his thoughts, his fear for her. Was she falling into the depression that had put her in the hospital? He didn't deserve to worry.

The tears dropped, and she promised herself to call him and put him at ease. She reached for a tissue, and there she found Luka standing at the foot of the tub. He looked impossibly handsome, holding a fluffy bath towel for her.

She stood up and let his eyes make love to her bubble covered body as she took slow, languid steps toward him. He held out his arms welcoming her return as he wrapped her in his strong arms.

"You're not alone, Babe."

She exhaled, leaning against him. No, she wasn't alone anymore. Luka's words brought a small measure of comfort. Then he added in a whisper next to her ear.

"CMT wants a meeting. I promised them tomorrow morning, ten-thirty sharp. You have to get out and carry on with your life."

She pulled back and looked up into his eyes. He was right. But she wasn't sure if she could.

He squeezed her tenderly, and his words gave her encouragement.

"You won't be alone. I'll be with you every step of the way." And then as if an afterthought added. "If you want me there."

She slid her arms up around his neck and pulled her face close she rested her cool cheek on his warm cheek.

"I do Luka, I do."

Luka stood holding her a long, long time and the strength of his big heart poured courage into her.

Holly agreed to the CMT meeting hoping money would

be involved. She had no idea how much money was in her bank account. She'd trusted that Brett would have seen to a generous severance payout, but how long could she live on her savings? Without a job, it wouldn't last long. And she wondered if a respectable law firm would take her seriously and hire an 'almost' lawyer that become notorious because she'd scandalously fucked a rock star?

Luka was right. Mourning the lost romance needed to end, and time to get on with her life. She took a deep breath and broke the moment.

She took hold of Luka's hand and walked out into her room. Her face lit up brightly. Luka waved his magical wand and changed the bed linens and made her bed. He'd generally restored order to the oversized room. By the door, sat two large bags filled, one of laundry and another of trash.

"Oh, that? Not another word. I'll drop off your laundry where I have mine done. I'll have them deliver it here. And I'll handle the rubbish."

"You take care of everything."

"I bloody well need to get you back on your feet. The surgeon tells me you've healed quicker than expected."

"Surgeon?"

"What we call the doctor."

She acknowledged his translation.

"Yes, I keep forgetting. I'm fine physically."

She looked around her room, noticing a gentle breeze blowing her curtains like billowing sails, and the soft scent of steamy vanilla rustled past her senses. She looked out into the garden filled with bright blue flowers against the backdrop of dark-green shrubs.

Yes, things were getting better.

Luka cleared away the Chinese food and then made a call.

She slipped into a dark green, cotton T-shirt, and black lace panties. She sat combing her knotted, waist-length hair.

He glanced at her saying. "I have a meeting in a half an hour," exhaled as he looked at her and as if to encouraged her to boost her sagging confidence.

"You look like a million dollars, Babe. You're going to be fine. You've given Kaine Walker enough of your life."

Luka was right.

As he walked out the door, he pulled a stack of tabloid newspapers from his briefcase and dropped them with a loud thud in a pile on the floor.

"Kaine's getting on with his life. And in case, you don't believe me. Read these. The message is clear."

Holly heard Luka fighting the press's onslaught of questions outside her fence as she picked up the tabloids. They were all foreign. Each was sprinkled with pictures of *Hurrikaine*, more to the point, Kaine with a variety of beautiful women surrounding him.

It was hard not to notice how everyone splashed a picture of her and Kaine on the cover. She couldn't read any of the foreign language print, but the pictures of the story were clear. Kaine had moved on with his life, London no more than yesterday's headline.

She cried most of the night, manically watching her videos and studied the tabloid photos. Her last thought before drifting to sleep.

I'm stronger than you think Kaine Walker. I will pull myself together.

The next morning Holly found the local tabloids delivered to her door weren't sympathetic either. Critics and readers speculated on what went wrong between Kaine and his mystery girlfriend to end the royal affair. She was used to her father, a newspaper editor/owner, ranting on about unethical yellow journalism. Therefore, she wasn't surprised. She sat and read on angry at their frightful theories that came nowhere near the truth.

For the second time in weeks, she sat soaking in her vanilla scented tub. She listened to "Now That I've Found You" on Kaine's gift, his CD player. She'd turned the radio mode blasting *Hurrikaine's* latest release. She bravely envisioned Kaine's riveting performance at Wembley Stadium.

It was then she realized this was the first time in weeks she visualized him without crying.

Perhaps the worst had passed?

Could it be she would go on with her own life?

She dressed in her Yves Saint Laurent black wool, tailored courtroom jacket with a mini skirt to match. The red rinse she put on her hair before leaving for London had long since faded away. She pulled her waist-long, blow-dried, thick, shiny, sable brown hair up into a black velvet clip, stepped into her black shoes, and remembered the black Prada heels she'd wore in London.

Thoughts of Friar Manor, Luka, the life-destroying kiss, Kaine and his subsequent heartbreak, and Sarah with her despicable threats passed fleetingly without the usual sting.

Perhaps it was true. The worst had passed.

She tempted fate by spraying on the Joy perfume she'd bought with Solange and wore for Kaine when Luka arrived on time.

He instantly erased the memory.

He stood tall, adorable, wearing a blue and white striped, cotton, collared, shirt with a movie studio cartoon logo over the pocket, below crisp, light blue Levi's, and white Hemp sports shoes.

She thought he was casual and attractive while he planted a quick inviting kiss on her cheek then complimented her stylist and professional attire.

She was happily surprised to see that Luka trimmed his long luscious hair to below his collar. He pulled off his white Eagles baseball cap and ran his fingers like a comb in his clean damp hair. His hair seemed to be one length with a bit of feathering to frame his gorgeous face. He shoved the cap back on his head.

"Not what I would have expected from the lady once dressed in London's finest black lace," he joked easily. "You are a professional."

Holly looked up and remembered Luka's explanation that the professional suit she'd worn backstage at the *Hurrikaine* concert, unknowingly placed her into a fierce competition. Both men entered into a rivalry of wanting her, to love her, to fight for a future with her.

She looked directly into Luka's sweet blue eyes, and she could clearly see how much he undeniable cared for her. She couldn't count the times in London, she was positively in love with him.

It was clear.

She'd suffered so much emotional pain it was difficult, if not impossible to believe she could ever have real feelings for him or anyone else, ever. At least, she would never have them as deep as her love was for Kaine.

This set-up wasn't fair to Luka.

She needed to do something.

She started to devise a plan.

She forced a tiny smile and placed her hand against his dear, sweet face.

"Let's start the rest of your life." He invited with a wink.

Luck was with them in the form of a break from the press.

They snuck out the back only to have Luka's Corvette followed by one tenacious newshound on a motorcycle. He tailed them all the way to the Wilshire area, into Beverly Hills, and then to a one-time major movie studio during the Golden Age of Hollywood, recently converted for CMT.

Even in her fog, Holly noted Luka was shown esteemed respect from everyone. She watched heads turn and heard the whispers. Everyone recognized her from the papers. How long would this turn-of-events interrupt her life?

Luka paused briefly in front of a well-coiffed secretary, and he instructed as he passed her without stopping.

"Tell Michael, I'm ready."

"He's been waiting, Mr. Hunter."

The secretary remarked as she hurried to step out of Luka's way.

He stuffed his baseball cap in his back pocket and every bit the executive led Holly inside to discover a larger executive office suite, richly furnished with a spectacular 180-degree view that reached all the way to Santa Monica Beach.

"Miss Hill," Michael announced, rising from his plush, black leather chair extending his hand toward her.

Michael Richmond, the gold nameplate read. She guessed to be in his mid-forties, a trim, healthy body and dressed in a dark blue, pinstriped Asset suit. His hair shiny black, well-trimmed and hung below his white, straight collar. His features dark, magnetically handsome to look at, but the most outstanding feature about Michael — his cologne. He wore a similar and as alluring a blend as Kaine's.

Holly found it challenging to concentrate on Michael's words. Flashes of being with Kaine all over London exploded in her mind. Far off in the distance, she heard Luka's muffled words construct a question.

"Are you interested? I would fancy showing you what you need. It would be part-time of course until we receive a surgeon's release form."

"Surgeon? Oh, yes, doctor. All right? I am sorry, Luka, I am a bit confused."

"Michael has offered you a position here at CMT as my personal assistant. Part-time of course until your surgeon releases you."

Holly sat surprised. Luka's assistant? What did she know about the music business? What she did know she wanted no more to do with, and besides, Luka's intentions were more than that of becoming her boss. She couldn't disappoint him again, and she wasn't ready for a personal commitment to anyone.

She needed to think fast.

She did need a change and the criminal law certainly held no future for her.

Holly looked over to Luka. He was coming to her rescue again. It would be a dangerous arrangement. And that was probably the reason she accepted. Luka was dangerous. The only man to make her forget her past with Kaine. On the practical side, this was also her only job offer.

That wasn't fair, she trusted and needed Luka more than any other person in her life.

Holly stood and offered her hand first to Michael and then to Luka. She continued to hold his hand because the look in Luka's eyes said something else was up, and she wasn't sure she wanted to be caught off guard.

She looked back to Michael and realized that the Chief Operating Officer of a major corporation had offered her a job usually handled by Human Resources. However, she'd been the Heart of the *Hurrikaine.* Perhaps Michael thought she needed a personal touch.

Holly glanced at Michael then to Luka wondering what was happening. But she would wait until they brought up the details on the subject.

Though impressed with their offer, and her suspicions aroused, she temporarily set them aside to reply, "I would be delighted to come aboard at CMT."

Michael displayed a satisfying grin, "Fantastic, then I shall notify personnel you will start. When?"

Holly looked to Luka.

He suggested and then winked.

"First of next week, but let's put her on the payroll as of the first of last month," he instructed glancing over to Michael. "Since she worked for CMT in London."

"Whatever you say, Luka," Michael affirmed and smiled again.

Luka stood, letting go of Holly's hand and offered his

arm.

"Let's celebrate. I shall fill you in on all the mystery of what I do to earn my keep around here."

Michael smiled as if waiting for a close up and boldly suggested.

"Why don't you take Holly out to your beach house in Malibu for the weekend to rest away from the press?"

Chapter Five

YOU WON'T SEE ME CRY

Beach house in Malibu? Holly choked back her surprise. "That's an excellent idea, Michael." Luka beamed.

"What do you say, Holly? Surf, the sun, moonlight walks along the sand? Sunsets? Sounds like what you need?"

"I think the beach and the sun are exactly what I need."

What she didn't say was, she did need the always handsome Luka to hold her, strolling along the shimmering beach drenched in the silver moonlight after the sun set. And that to stroll with him in the moonlight sounded perfectly divine, perfect as all of her internal systems went off at the same time warning — danger.

It was true.

He's dangerous, hopefully, dangerous enough to make her forget.

"Smashing, let's go!" He urged quickly.

His sunny smile erasing any doubts creeping into her mind.

Holly walked next to Luka as they strolled down the long

corridor, she a half-step behind him. She admired his sun-streaked, collar length hair, swinging back and forth in the invisible wind with each step of his confident gait. Every woman he passed, their eyes said it all, they dreamed of touching him. And then they turned their blazing gaze to stare at her, and she read the same story in each pair of eyes, all blind with envy.

There were things that didn't change.

Apparently, Luka had a house in Malibu. Who was Luka Hunter? She was ashamed to admit she was starting to be drawn in a bit more because each twist was more intriguing than the last. How complicated everything became in Luka's world. He'd been a mystery man for too long. She knew nothing of his past except that he had circled the globe with *Hurrikaine* for all of his adult life. She didn't know where he called home or if he had any family. And each new piece of the puzzle to Luka always surprised her. He wasn't a man given to speaking lines to her, as she'd once believed. He had been the center of the *Hurrikaine* music machine, and it was clear he wasn't the CMT representative. Luka was an executive that carried a lot of power and prestige at CMT.

Hadn't Kaine said?

He must be powerful to scrap the video script at the last minute and rewrite it to include you?

And in spite of the California casual wardrobe, he drove a brand new Corvette and owned a beach house at Malibu? Maybe they were both leased?

Who the hell was Luka Hunter?

Luka stopped at the elevator, but she was deep in thought. Holly didn't stop in time, and she crashed into his tall, lean body. She reached out to grab a hold of him as she lost her balance. She pressed against him as he protectively grabbed her elbow to hold her steady.

He looked down, deep into her eyes and he parted his lips showing her his bright white teeth and smiled a sexy smile that made her surrender.

"Holding you in my arms like this was how this all started. It's a perfect way to start our new life together."

Together!

His encouraging words raised her hopes, yet all the warning sounds blasted.

Holly's first excursion out quickly exhausted her, but quickly concealed. She was quietly relieved Luka was taking her far away from the stifling Santa Ana winds to the beach.

She'd grown up in Santa Barbara, and always loved the calm, beautiful, cool, white-tipped waves playfully lapping at her bare toes while she walked along the water's edge. She threw her head back and let the wind comb her hair, happily anticipating the healing effect of the ocean's serene atmosphere would have on her.

Luka drove up the wooded, curving lane in Laurel Canyon, high above the Sunset Strip and parked on the back street behind her cottage. They were in luck, only one vulture perched.

She watched as the newshound quickly clicked off a roll of film before she made it to her gate. She didn't care anymore because soon she would be free of press and depression for two whole days.

Holly slipped into a pair of blood-red colored walking shorts and a white, scooped neck, lace-trimmed camisole. She tied her laces on her white running shoes and then packed her LV KeepAll, recalling it was a gift from Kaine, and then noticed the knot growing hard in her stomach.

She wondered if Luka would make her forget Kaine this time. And the thought compelled her to look over at him, to study him.

Yes, definitely. Only Luka Hunter could do that.

Luka jetted along Sunset Blvd., driving his Corvette past the young, scruffy vendors selling tour maps to the stars' homes. He sped past the University and the seafood restaurant at the corner of Pacific Coast Highway and Sunset Blvd. The cool, sea breeze blew on her face. A pleasant alternative to the hellish Santa Ana winds assaulting L.A. that brought record-breaking temperatures.

She spent the last of the afternoon holding the dangerous Luka Hunter's soft hand, strolling up and down the cool sparkling sand while he spoke to half of L.A., on his phone. She watched the water sparkle as the blazing sun dipped behind the oceans white-capped waves. S

Holly sighed releasing a deep breath of fresh air. She relaxed for the first time in weeks. When Luka hung up for what seemed like the hundredth time, he pulled her to him. The strong sea breeze blew their hair and caressed their faces. He placed her in front of him, and they watched the golden globe make its final descent.

"Another sunset together," she said almost cooing, then exhaled.

"One of thousands, Babe," he reassured her.

She leaned back against him. There were worse fates in the world than being with this charming Englishman that happens to act as if a man who cared deeply for her.

Holly welcomed his soothing, subtle charm washing over her, quietly, bringing her comfort and safety. And yes, grateful that Luka gave her the gift of time.

She glanced down to see a thin mist of fog dancing with her feet as Luka hugged her quickly.

"Time to look for supper."

Holly lingered over herbal iced tea. They sat in a dark corner of a restaurant owned by a 1950s famous movie star tucked away high in the Malibu Hills. Next to the window with a spectacular ocean view. But the best view sat across from her. Luka made her laugh, and it was the first time in a long time that she'd laughed. It was true. She smiled and giggled at his horrible jokes and for the time being she did not ache somewhere on her body, especially in her heart. Luka was doing what he did best weaving her broken heart back together.

She hadn't heard a *Hurrikaine* song during her outing. Never saw a newspaper photograph or media photographers ready to hound her for answers she didn't have. After the golden-rimmed, California sun. It's had settled down for the evening, the moon arrived as a brilliant silver crescent, the only purpose — shower Luka with moonlight. Its job was well done because he was breathtaking.

His amazing blue eyes sparkled as he focused on her every move. She wanted to reach out and touch his face as the reflection of the candlelight, wanting to taste his full, succulent lips fresh from a run of his tongue across them. Certainly, he was what the poets meant by an ethereal looking man, every feature perfect, too handsome for words to describe.

While he sat holding her hand, he spoke of nothing at all. He held her hand when he walked her to his convertible. He leaned close, so close and the cool breeze blew his hair back off his neck. And for the first time in such a long time, she filled with an enthusiastic desire for him. The delicious need for him so intense it urged her to go up on her tiptoes, up close enough to place her lips on his.

But she didn't dare.

She hadn't kissed Luka in weeks. She knew she wouldn't stop at one of his luscious, dreamy kisses, magical kisses that would whisk her away to their secret place where he would confirm his private affection for her. No, she wasn't strong enough to kiss Luka Hunter yet. She rested her head on his shoulder and sighed. The brisk but carefree sea breeze tossed her long hair as he drove further up the coastline. Eventually, Luka pulled up to the entrance of the Malibu Colony.

"Good evening Mr. Hunter, beautiful night." The guard politely greeted and then looked up at the clear sky.

Luka nodded yes and drove past the gate onto the exclusive, star-studded property. Luka was taking her home with him. He'd never taken her anywhere he stayed in London.

He pulled up to a three-story, white Mediterranean-styled house any architect would be proud to have built. Settled inside, Luka showed her around the house. She was delighted to find the spacious home comfortably decorated with subtle, natural designs. The color palette warm pastels of greens, oranges, and blues, the furnishings bleached rattan. The spectacular, high gloss hardwood floors were covered with assorted scatterings of wool rugs.

They made small talk until the clock struck midnight. She remembered London, and how they'd called 'Midnight' their special time.

Apparently, so did Luka.

"It's midnight Babe," Luka smiled and moved closer.

She saw his tongue slip between his lips and leave a wet trail to make them glisten.

His eyelids hung half hooded but not with passion, instead, filled with gentleness. Luka reached out for her, inviting her into his embrace.

She stepped into his arms as natural as taking a breath.

He embraced her as if a fragile prize.

Holly snuggled into his chest that rose and fell with each breath. He held her steady against him, his cheek with a day's beard, rubbed against the side of her forehead. But his lips did not seek hers. The disappointment crushed her.

"You need rest, Babe. There's a large, comfortable guest suite down the hall on the left, with a spectacular view of the beach. Your things are there. I'm upstairs on the opposite side at the back of the house."

She announced with an edge of disappointment, "You don't have to go so far away from me. I trust you."

"You would, Babe." He kissed her on top of her head.

"Go, straightaway before I change the sleeping arrangements."

She stepped back and looked at him. Her eyes must be telling him that she did adore him.

"You're an amazingly special man Luka Hunter. I don't deserve you."

He cocked his head to the side and his long hair cascade

to the side. His face lit up with a magnificent smile that would charm the universe.

"It's the other way around, Babe."

He turned and walked away.

Luka did not kiss her good night.

She crawled out of bed to sit by the window and watched the waves carry her thoughts thousands of miles away. She wiped away her tears. She was so lonely. All she saw in her mind's eye was the brooding, handsome face, his spectacular blue eyes, and his luscious dark hair. And, of course, his bracket dimples that hugged his perfect smile. And she didn't want to get started on those luscious kissable lips.

Kaine.

She wiped away her tears.

Holly awoke the next morning more rested than she would have anticipated. She settled into an easy rhythm with Luka. He was impossibly companionable and attentive. And when he threw a surprise barbecue that evening to introduce her to the famous names in Malibu Colony, she was amazed she'd found the time to long for Kaine. But she had. She was ashamed to admit it, but when she'd watched the others so easy with each other, sharing anecdotes and discussing show business, how much she yearned for Kaine. They had the good manners not to mention Kaine. Though Luka pointed out, they were aware that she'd carried the title of the Heart of the *Hurrikaine.*

Even in Malibu, they had tabloids.

She smiled quickly again, missing Kaine, his tall body standing next to her. She wished for the ease of his gentle touch like when she placed her hand in the crook of his arm when shy.

And later, in the dark, listening to the clock chime midnight, she lay awake, alone. She listened to the rhythmic waves roll in one after the other until she scolded herself. She needed to stop these obsessive thoughts of Kaine that would certainly destroy her.

But how to make them cease?

Chapter Six

SHE'S WAITING

Holly awoke mired in gray clouds of sadness, the waves of melancholy intent on smothering her.

She lay twisted around a large down-filled pillow. Unmercifully, she'd dreamt of Kaine again. His memory, the strongest so far. The aroma of his intoxicating scent lingered as the taste of him.

She shook the moments from her thoughts because it was time for the morning challenge. The recurring waves of queasiness forced her from the warm, cocooned memories of Kaine to her knees in front of the cold, porcelain commode. The third morning in a row she'd awoke with a queasy stomach. Would it ever end? She made a mental note to tell the doctor when she saw him later in the week for a follow-up appointment. Holly rinsed the foul bile from her mouth and then lingered for a moment to settle her stomach.

Soon she was digging into her LV KeepAll. She pulled out a black bikini to christen the shores of Malibu. She slipped her arms into a soft blue denim shirt and wandered out to the lanai.

She hesitated.

She saw Luka first.

He stood quietly lost in reflective thoughts, staring out to sea. Vintage blues, raw and primal, was crooning about love in the background. The singer's lyrics hung heavy in the air about wanting to make love. The sight of Luka instantly sapped all the air from her lungs because every damn inch of his gorgeous body enticed her.

Luka was casually leaning against the sliding glass door. His arms folded across his chest, his legs crossed at the ankles, wearing nothing but a simple pair of black Levi's cutoffs, that hung too low on his slim hips.

Her heart gave way because he may as well have been Zeus, god of the heavens himself. The last time she'd seen Luka this naked had been in her hotel room the last night in London.

Holly bit her bottom lip picturing how the damned sheet had been draped across his lap to conceal him as the Levi's did. How maddening. She wanted to see the hardness of him. She must be healing. Doing better at least because it was definitely time to see Luka naked.

Luka turned as he heard Holly enter the room. He relaxed his stance and took a step closer to her.

Holly sucked in a quick breath. Luka Hunter was more striking than any movie star in the colony was. His blond hair was pulled back into a loose tail while long, thick locks hung alongside his cheeks.

"Sleep well, Luv?" He inquired softly, his voice thick and sexy.

The hard blow landed in her stomach as his voice, so

alluring demanded of all of her attention. She narrowed her eyes. It was refreshing to yearn to touch him.

"Yes, thank you." She lied.

"Breakfast? I have squeezed fresh orange juice, blueberry muffins are warm from the bakery, or there's sliced fresh pineapple if you prefer." He looked up at her when she didn't move. "What is it, Babe? Something wrong?"

Why lie?

"You, Luka."

"Me? What have I done?" His voice rose quickly to a high pitch, first laced with innocence and then filled with concern.

"Nothing Luka." Her voice grew weak. "That's it. You're perfect in every way, and I'm grateful you are here with me."

Luka quickly released his sunny smile and sighed a quick breath of relief. Then he surprised her with his response.

"I'm glad to hear those words. I feel the same way."

He flashed her one of his mischievous smiles meant to block out the sun then bent slightly at the waist so gentlemanly.

But her eyes never left his bare chest. She watched the muscles move as he poured her juice into a crystal glass.

Hypnotized.

Frozen to that spot by his powerful masculinity.

Luka stepped around the table and gently pressed his warm lips against her cheek. "Good morning, Babe," he greeted smoothly, thick and husky like he'd spent the long night showing her how to delight him, pleasure him, and enjoy him.

She closed her eyes. The fresh-showered scent of him

forced the delicious picture of him slipping out of his cutoffs.
All the while a fresh, gentle breeze blew his sexy scent all
about her like a Voodoo spell cast to drive her wild.

She opened her eyes as he passed her. His damp hair
shimmered in the bright Malibu sunlight as he handed her the
fruit platter. It was starting to happen again, losing her
defenses, no wall of pain to keep her from Luka. No media to
hound her. No ghost of Kaine to step between them. This was
how it would be to be alone with Luka. What a wise man he
was to take her away from everything and everyone she knew.
No distractions, only the one — how to get him naked.

Luka slipped his arm around Holly's waist and pulled her
beside him. When he touched her, his heat radiated like
blistering sunburn. She summoned her courage. She needed to
stand her ground — let him seduce her as his hips pressed
hers.

Luka was growing aroused, or not!

"Come here, Babe. It's a beautiful morning. If you prefer,
we'll eat out here. And if you are well enough, later I'll take
you on an adventure."

"Adventure?" She exclaimed full of excitement raising
her eyebrows.

"Great, I can't remember the last time I was offered such
an intriguing invitation."

"Your injuries giving you any more trouble?"

No, for once, it wasn't her injuries. It was the
overwhelming thought of getting him out of his Levi's. But
she was quick to note he was inquiring about her physical
progress. She wouldn't make love with him in those last days
in London, first, because she had been too badly bruised and

battered by Sarah, *that bitch,* she'd decided to add. And second, she decided in London, to say good-bye to him, no longer believing she could have any relationship with him based on her betrayal to Kaine — with him. And lastly, the one she didn't want to remember was how Luka wanted to wait.

"No, I'm well, Luka," she emphasized the word 'well.'

"The fear and pain have disappeared. I have you, and your incredibly handsome smile to brighten my days. I believe the worst is over, Luka."

"Well." He smiled brightly showing his straight white, movie star teeth. "That is bloody good news."

The hint of excitement in his voice intrigued her. A number of possibilities might fill this day. She inhaled a deep breath to fortify her.

Luka whistled a snappy melody to follow the lyrics of the song and kept busy moving the breakfast outside to the lanai.

But Holly watched him with the interest of a starved animal sizing up its prey. She studied the way each muscle moved under the tight skin on his back when he reached up for a pitcher. The many ways his bronzed skin rippled over his ribs when he stretched and twisted at the waist to pick up the crystal glasses. How his thighs were long, his legs lean, and his calves shapely. She noticed a light covering of sparkling, light-brown hair along his feet and toes that looked like he'd sat for a recent pedicure. He took such good care of himself. His aristocratic background looked smashing on Luka. He wore his English manners with grace and elegance. Each step, he took the muscles in his legs pulled tight and taut, and that meant there'd be no stopping the erotic thoughts erupting to stoke the fires of her imagination.

Luka, she sighed.

A sudden loud beep captured Luka's attention. He sprinted to retrieved the last muffin from the microwave oven and dropped it on a saucer. He leaned back against the tiled counter and crossed his legs at the ankles.

Holly reached out. Her hand trembled as she picked up the tableware. She closed her eyes to gain strength, knowing when they opened them she'd be looking at Luka's firm, trim abdomen.

She opened them.

Stunning.

His rippling skin covered the rungs of his ribs, begging Holly to touch him. Her hungry eye followed the line of glistening light brown hair tucked under the waistband of Luka's cutoffs that hung below the tan line on his slim hips. Then her eyes rested comfortably on the fullness of his pants. She smiled, pleased with his reaction to her. He, too, must like what he saw. She watched him grow, remembering his full shape and size.

Holly smiled as she reminisced about how beautiful that wondrous part of his body was. Holly smiled wider, watching him strain against the cloth of his pants tempting her to stroke him.

Oh, yes, they both wanted the same thing. On the floor suited her. Hadn't he called it "fucking her brains out"? But she knew Luka well enough to know the seduction had begun in London. He wouldn't hurry. This invitation would take hours, probably days. Her mind sprinted wondering where the moment would be when Luka finally decided to bury himself in her.

Luka was so close. Close enough to touch him, to feel him grow hard in her hand. Holly grabbed a long, soulful breath as the old lustful feelings for Luka blasted her mind and then her body, pushing her breath a bit quicker. How ridiculous she'd been, he was impossible to resist.

He knew that.

And Kaine knew that.

And now, she knew that.

Holly drew in another ragged breath and shook her head.

How much longer would she be able to deny herself the undiluted pleasures of Luka? She hoped she wouldn't have to beg.

"Come, everything's ready." He summoned softly flashing another one of his sunny, soul piercing smiles.

"Let's eat."

Holly covered her stomach with her palm to block the instant rise of nausea assaulting her, picturing swallowing a slice of pineapple. It had been such a long time since she'd been this well, healthy, or as perky as Luka seemed. And she didn't want to do anything to change her rejuvenated spirits.

"You have made a beautiful breakfast and have remembered every detail. But I'll have juice. Unfortunately, I'm not that hungry."

He flashed his warm smile, and while the words seemed to lace his lips, he did not ask her any questions. His beautiful blue eyes were fighting to extinguish his worry.

After a quiet, meditative brunch her thoughts drifted to a refreshing dip in the ocean to calm her raging desires. But she could tell by the coy smile on his face, his idea was better.

Luka gathered the glasses in one hand, hers in his other. He led her out onto the warm sand where he laid out a large beach towel. He pulled her down with him to soak in the sun's healing rays and stretched out on the warm sand inches from her. He leaned back to sip his orange juice.

They lay comfortably chatting about CMT, to ease the exploding sexual tension. Luka filled her in on her new duties. She barely listened to his droning words because far off in the distance her heart had been viciously recaptured.

Without warning or mercy, her mind zeroed in on "Moments of a Memory" and she heard Kaine singing his heart out from a neighbor's house. She wanted to cover her ears and scream. She remembered him in the hotel suite shower, naked, singing the song to her. The reminder wasn't fair, but then, if she'd never cheated, she would be in Paris with him on her honeymoon. Instead, Kaine reminded her of her deceit and unfaithfulness with Luka.

And here she was again — with him!

But this was supposed to be her time to heal — her time to forget.

Would there always be a crushing reminder? Would she never be free? Could she ever hide from Kaine Walker? Why had she ever fallen in love with him?

Maybe if Kaine hadn't been able to change her whole world, or shown her a new life. Perhaps she would not have fallen into this torturous Hell of loving him, hating him, missing him, wanting Luka to murder the memory of him.

Holly gazed helplessly into Luka's beautiful blue eyes, longing to see Kaine's. Suddenly, her heart shattered, as a burning guilt flooded her.

"I'm sorry Luka," she apologized as she bolted up and shook her head.

Holly took her turn to stare out at the ocean, watching the white-tipped waves rolling in one after the other a coward, too afraid to look at Luka when she'd finished her sentence. "I get flashbacks of London."

"I understand," he spoke sympathetically. "I have them too. Sometimes London creeps into my dreams."

"Kaine … comes to me while I'm asleep … when I can't fight him," she hesitantly admitted.

"I'm here, Babe. But I can only keep the flesh and blood of him away from you. The rest you'll have to deal with on your own."

Holly shook her head in agreement. And before she could stop the tiny tear from escaping, Luka took a hold of her hand. To her disappointment, there was no fiery exchange, no sexual suggestion — his grip, more protective.

Luka spoke quietly, almost in a whisper. "Babe, let's go for a walk."

Luka stood straight and tall.

Holly moved upward onto both knees and paused to avoid looking straight at his strong promise to make mind bend love. He was next to her face so close to her.

She looked skyward as he pulled her up close beside him. She reached for the handsome face of her dear friend, gazing into his soft, caring eyes, wondering if she would ever be able to call him her lover. Or, would Kaine always prevent that?

Luka, his beautiful face scarred from the marks of Kaine. The gash reminded her every time she looked at Luka that Kaine vented his rage and jealousy on Luka — because of her.

It was in these stolen moments that she'd found peace with Luka. She whispered as she stood up next to him.

"I'm so grateful for you Luka."

He gently swept her into his warm, sun-kissed arms without a moment's hesitation. She naturally filled in the curves of his body. The warm scent of him oiled with tropically scented sunscreen drew her closer. Her head spun from the sudden return of her overpowering attraction to him.

He paused, looking at her as if waiting for something.

She shuddered with a flash of fear that threatened to steal her fleeting peace. What was he thinking? What bombshell was he preparing to drop?

"I don't want you to think about Kaine when you are with me. I made you forget him in London. I can do it. But you have to let me Holly."

How much Holly wanted his words to be true. She desperately pressed her breasts to Luka's chest. Shoved her hips into him and wrapped her leg around his. Holly told him she would try with every fiber in her body. Then she told him with her eyes. She would forget Kaine. She pushed herself up to his pink lips. Lips so luscious she wanted to kiss them and then suck them; run her tongue over them, over and over again, knowing she would never have her fill.

Luka surprised her by accepting her amorous response, allowing his mouth a breath away from hers.

She closed her eyes as he closed the gap and then pressed her lips lightly, too lightly for the raging lust exploding inside her. But Luka's kiss was easy. She couldn't hold back and tested his restraint by running her tongue along the seam of his lips. She wanted to taste of Luka.

He opened his mouth and covered hers.

She dipped into the warm chamber of his kiss.

Mmmmm ...to kiss Luka brought the most wondrous sensations.

This man brought years of global travel to his mesmerizing kiss. And what a masterful kiss it was. His arms pulled her to him carefully making sure not to hurt her as he shared his powerful kiss — a man's kiss.

Luka Hunter grew more forceful, demanding and reminding her again of his vast experience and deep passion. He crawled deeper into her mouth kissing her the way she loved as if he'd been her only teacher.

How did he manage to keep his deepest feelings in check was a mystery? Deeper he kissed her, waving his magician's wand transporting her to the private place he had shown her in London. His breath ran ragged as all the pent-up passions he held restrained for her these past weeks flowed freely.

It took all of Holly's strength to keep up with Luka. But she would, she vowed to and then some. Her mind was empty as she pressed against Luka wanting him blindly. Exactly like the first moments, she met him in London when he was the most beautiful and desirable man alive.

Luka's soothing hands slipped up and down her oiled body. Strong hands that knew every inch of her. Creative hands that reinvented her when he dressed her scandalously, in her first music video. And sensitive hands that had tended to her wounds and broken spirit. Sexy, experienced hands that claimed they wanted to make love to her and make her scream.

Finally, finally!

She would enjoy the perfect joy and splendor of Luka. She wanted him to transform her into his lover. To create a place where she could love and learn from him, all of his sensual tricks and fantasies. To be lost in the magic of his talented hands. To be enchanted by the magician as he touched her everywhere, devouring her.

Luka's rush of hot, moist kisses penetrated the flimsy veil of pain, melting her resolve and firing her desire, this was Luka. She leaned into his golden chest, pushing her arms up, sliding them up his hot slippery back. His silky blond hair fell out of the tied restriction dropped like a shimmering waterfall into her shoulders tickling her like a spray of water drops. His skillful fingers tugged behind her back, nimbly untying the top of her swimsuit and it fell between them.

Luka pulled it out and dropped it onto the sand. All the while, he kept kissing her, draining the last of her strength from her being.

Holly stood out in the open for the entire world to watch as she forgot Luka masterfully removed her bikini top during a moment of heated passion. He never had before, and her only thought was she'd finally have Luka. The powerful, lusty pictures she envisioned caused her light-headedness to the point she feared she'd faint. She quivered as his hand slide around her marking a trail of tingling sensations up and over her stomach to where he stopped to tantalize her bare sun-kissed breasts.

She moved in closer and all of her body burned on fire. But mostly the fire blasted from deep below her belly. She quaked as his thumb rubbed across her nipples. They grew hard from sparking lust like a flint to a keg of kerosene. She slipped her thigh higher over one of his legs.

He pushed his ready manhood into her, rubbing her with long, luscious strokes. Finally, she would have him, no one to interrupt them. No ghost to haunt her. And all of Luka's demons from his painful past seemed quiet for the moment.

It was time.

Holly slid her hand up the side of his neck fanning her fingers into his silky hair. She followed the hard curve of his head, massaging his skin and weaving her fingers in and out of his hair. She didn't care where she was or who watched. She was with Luka, and he was making her forget. She surrendered to Luka's enchanting touch, compelling her up and onto tiptoes to kiss him harder, deeper losing herself in their exploding passion.

Please, Luka, before I lose my courage, she thought frantically.

As if reading her mind Luka pulled away and allowed the sun to slip in drenching her tender breasts with heat. Luka's eyes burned with lust and passion as he drank in the sight of her full creamy breasts and rosy-tipped nipples. He hesitated and swallowed and as his words flowed, she was sure she didn't want to listen to them. "Holly, I've cared for you since the first moment I saw you in London. The hardest thing I've ever done was to hand you over to that bloody sod, Kaine. After everything that's happened, I hope you can trust me. When you told me the last day in London that you loved me that was the happiest moment, I've experienced in a long time. I hope you believe I'd do anything for you and that you can trust me."

Luka, no.

Holly didn't want the pressure or the commitment. She hadn't meant that she loved him, the way he was speaking. It wasn't and never could be the forever love she'd experienced with Kaine. She didn't have the words to promise she wouldn't hurt him sometime in the future — if Kaine came back. How she hated herself for admitting that. The truth was grinding in her stomach. And his eyes said, tell me something? It was her turn to confess her feelings because his eyes were screaming they cracking under the silence.

Holly started the broken sentence. "I do believe you Luka … and I trust you. And I care deeply about you. But…." She started to hesitate, knowing it was wrong to finish her sentence. She grabbed at any passing thought to balance the rejection. "… but … a different way from Kaine. You've been so good to me during the fiasco with Kaine and then my depression. But if you want the truth? I'm confused Luka. I can't lie to you. It would only confuse things more. I don't have rational words to explain my irrational feelings other than being addicted and coming off a drug. One minute I'm sure I can beat it. The next I crave Kaine in a way that hurts me to admit to you. It's not fair to you my dear sweet Luka."

She placed her hands on the sides of his freshly shaven, smooth face.

"I'm with you. You are my man with the angel eyes. You will always be my angel eyes. Please, I'm with you. I don't want to speak of Kaine again."

Luka's smile did not shine with a victory. His voice stayed even but weighted with the sharp edge of disappointment.

"Agreed," he responded without resolve.

"But it's important you realized that after all you've

bloody well been subjected to the fact that you haven't said no and sent me away. Well, Babe, I can wait. I'll give you time."

Something changed between them.

She did not confess she loved him. Neither did he.

His magical way of being one-step ahead of her always brought her comfort. She smiled at his humility. As if, she could ever say no to Luka. Hasn't that always been the problem? Now wasn't the time to point that out to him. Time was what she needed, lots of time with the steady, reliable, sexy Luka Hunter with no reminders of Kaine, one sunset after another with a naked Luka. He alone would capture her complete attention and eventually make her forget. Her future depended on it.

"Forget London," he growled.

She leaned deeper into Luka's protective embrace, inviting him to work his magic again.

He followed her lead spreading a sweet trail of soft kisses down the long line of her neck to her chest. Suddenly he stopped and stood up straight. She looked up into his blue eyes. Eyes that said, today he would make love to her today if she'd let him. Lost in his eyes, endless sky-blue eyes, she fought the intruding thought.

Never free, never free from those eyes.

They glowed bright blue today, like Kaine's.

There he was again!

Holly tried to smile to cover her dark thoughts. What had she ever done to deserve Luka's devotion? She leaned forward once again to kiss him deeply giving him permission to proceed, warning the ghost of Kaine if he stayed around he would witness her complete surrender to Luka.

The dark haired ghost took a step back.

Luka placed his arm behind her legs and picked her up in his strong sun-kissed arms.

She opened her lust, glazed eyes to see his glistening sun-streaked hair swaying along his shoulders. She pulled back a long, thick lock of his hair, exposing his long, streamlined neck, begging to be kissed as he carried her up on the lanai.

He dropped to his knees behind a row of medium-height potted plants that blocked the offshore breeze. The sun's rays beat down hot and oppressive.

Holly stretched out on the soft lounge chaise, welcoming, absorbing the sun's fiery rays. Luka took great strides to make her comfortable. Then he unbuttoned the top button and then unzipped his cut-off Levi's.

He sent the call to her.

Soon.

He dropped them.

She heard a light thud. And there for all to see was the most gorgeous man alive. Luka with all of his love ready, willing to show her how much he loved her, wanted her. And, how the madness of waiting for her burned for weeks.

He moved closer.

She grabbed a breath.

He was shockingly beautiful. His love and lust flashed brilliantly in his eyes. He was coming for her as everyone predicted. He always got what he wanted, and that was she.

Well, he was here — he'd arrived.

She was his for the taking.

He evenly rested the weight of his glorious, naked body on top of hers. A few thoughts ran about in her mind. She busied herself memorizing every inch of Luka's lovely face. Each time she looked at those eyes, his face, he amazed her. She always saw something different, something unique to Luka. He was such an amazing creation. How many times was she alone with Luka? Too many, but, this time, was different. This time, she would make beautiful and wondrous love with him.

Holly kissed Luka deeply, pushing Kaine another step backward. She ignored the fact that Luka wasn't the *one*. Holly's mind emptied again. She allowed herself the exquisite joy recalling Luka's exciting body, his gentle touch, his powerful love.

His perfect nude body pressed hers exciting her. She came alive as Luka's smooth manicured fingertips roamed freely over her body. He touched her wherever he pleased. No longer concerned he may hurt her. Pleasure drove his intentions and filled his mind.

Luka stopped to linger and then deliberately slipped his hands over her tropically scented body.

At long last, after he massaged every muscle at arm's length. His hand slid inside her thong.

Holly realized Luka was locked in heavy combat with Kaine.

Luka owned the apparent edge as his fingers worked their magic casting the enchantment, loving her as only he could.

The ghost of Kaine lingered, threatening to leave, promising to return, as Luka kissed her breast and then suckled her nipple.

Kaine moved farther away, to the far-reaching vistas of her mind. Holly was barely able to see his willowy shadow, his shoulders hunched as he whirled around and vanished into the fog.

Luka did it again, wiped her final thought of Kaine from her memory. She heard his enticing words floating on clouds praising her.

"You're bloody beautiful, Babe. We have the whole day to ourselves. Let me show you how special you are to me."

Whole day? Making love with Luka???

The war ended, finally.

Holly forgot Kaine as her passion detonated for Luka. Her body responded perfectly to Luka's masterful loving. Her hands ravaged his hair and then hungrily sought to touch his strong, well-defined shoulders down his taut, muscular back squeezing him tightly. Fired with an exploding lust for him, driven by trust, she relaxed under his protection and encouraged her reckless hand to continue its mission, down to where she found him waiting.

Hummm, patient, strong, hard as iron.

With Luka's help, Holly squirmed free of her thong as he unhooked the sides. Finally, she was naked too. She opened her legs to invite his talent … to enjoy his fingers itching with lust and desire, remembering his touch, ready to receive unimaginable pleasure.

"Hurry, hurry."

The words poured quickly, already close to her release. She hadn't realized how aroused by him she had become … all the days and hours of Luka's masterful seduction. She took a quick breath as he twisted swiftly to protect himself. He slid up her oiled body. The weight of him evenly distributed lying naked on her.

A perfect fit.

Luka paused.

Too late.

She'd beg if he wanted. She needed him to enter her, to fill her, to move in and out of her, showing her his incredible strength and durability.

Holly didn't notice the unwavering shadow's return.

Urgently, she whispered into Luka's ear.

"Now.

"Now. Kaine.

" ... I love you."

Chapter Seven

UNTIL I FALL AWAY

Any moment! Holly waited an incredibly long time for this spellbinding moment with Luka — the ultimate magic man — the only man able to wipe away Kaine. *Hurry.*

Holly dug her fingertips into Luka's back, pulling him into her. The sound of the distant waves crashed on the shoreline.

What was happening?

Why was Luka waiting?

"No, don't!" She cried out, clinging even tighter to Luka, pulling him closer as if to climb inside his skin.

"Now!" She insisted.

There was only one response.

Luka's tall, lean body relaxed and then pulled away.

Holly shivered as a cold, unnerving chill slipped under her skin. She opened her half hooded eyes.

Holly slammed them shut, blinded by the bright sun. She covered her eyes barely able to see the opaque outline of his shadow. All she saw were his golden strands of hair hanging long, touching her face. And if the harsh expression on his face hadn't surprised her, the hair tickling her face would have brought a smile to her.

"What's wrong?" She managed between pulling short breaths, knowing this wave of rejection building would be hard to fight and would leave her broken and filled with shame.

Holly would do anything Luka wanted.

Confess.

Beg.

Lie.

If only he would release his passion for her.

Finally, Luka's husky voice broke the crushing silence. His British accent flowed easily then exploded into a low indignant tone.

"I'm not bloody Kaine!"

"Of course, you're not. Why on Earth would you mention him?" She reached up and took hold of one long lock of his hair and draped it behind his ear as if to dismiss his ridiculous reply.

In a quiet voice, even tone Luka repeated her stinging words.

"Now ... Now ... Kaine. I love you...."

All of Holly's passion instantly drained into the black abyss of shame. She'd fooled herself again and this time at Luka's expense.

"Can't you forgive me?" She quickly pleaded.

She didn't need to explain anymore. She glanced away from his sad blue eyes where she caught a glimpse of him trying to hide his pain and rejection.

He surprised her with his quick response.

"It's my fault, Holly. I've rushed you. How could I

reasonably expect you to put aside your sincere feelings for Kaine, to please me? I've been a selfish lout, and I deserve this.

"That's why I want us to find a way to heal the past and build a new future. It's hard for me to admit, but you fell hard for Kaine, that bloody bastard. And it's going to take you more time than I expected to examine your true feelings.

"Try to remember this. You can trust me. I won't rush you. And I promise I won't do this again. Not until you're ready."

His speech, eloquent, but his eyes betrayed him as he looked away. His eyes glistened, and they could not cloak the anger that lay behind his eyes.

Holly didn't want him to stop. She wanted him to fight the ghost with her — to banish Kaine and start fresh. She watched Luka tear his tender love from her and hide it deep in his heart. Her tears of shame for betraying Luka were too strong to hold back.

"Don't look at me with those eyes," he advised, and then moved away from her again. He'd stood quickly, and before she drank in the exquisite sight of him, he sprinted down the steps of the lanai.

Holly bolted up to watch as his naked body ran across the gleaming sands and straight into the sparkling white-capped waves of the Pacific Ocean. Luka, her beautiful Luka, left her to drown in a pool of dreadful feelings, blaming herself for everything.

"Why can't I turn to Luka and love him? He's the good one. He's the one with the real love."

Holly wiped the chiding tears from her cheeks watching

Luka's head bobbing on top of the ocean's foaming white curls as he worked his passion for her from his body. She lay back, stunned, unable to process words, thoughts, anything, or cover her naked body. But the warm sun's rays brought healing.

Holly started to develop a plan.

When Luka returned, she would explain to Luka the ways she would change, how she would love him. Tell him she loved him lavishing her with his kisses, touching her with his magical hands and have him deep inside her.

She wondered why the awful twists of events happened.

The sun's rays continued as a potent remedy. The heat wrapped her body as a warm healing salve rubbed on her naked body draining a handful of the guilt from her.

After nursing her upset nerves with a sparkling mineral water, she pulled on an opaque gold cover-up that complimented her skin tone.

To quiet her thoughts, she'd focused on preparing a meal and chopped red and green peppers, heated water for pasta, and then lightly seasoned the sourdough bread.

Holly waited for Luka's return and opened another mineral water. Out on the lanai, she set the wrought iron glass table with beautiful Lomagé tableware while listening to the torch singer declare she was the only one.

Holly waited … chopping … and tossing.

She waited.

Chapter Eight

RUN

True to his word, Luka kept his distance. He'd taken the side stairs inside the house. He must have showered because when he descended the stairs, his hair was wet and pulled back in a tail. The scent of herbal shampoo was strong.

Luka was an impressive sight. He'd changed into a white cotton shirt left unbuttoned, wore baggy, white cotton trousers that hung low on his hips and stood barefooted.

Stunning.

But his eyes never met hers.

What was worse, he remained silent during dinner. All the while, her mind whirled asking herself if she had destroyed their future.

Luka, unbelievably kind, generous, considerate and sensitive, and let's not forget brave, and strong. He sounded too much like her hero. And if he were smart, he would run as fast as he could from her.

But he wouldn't.

No one treated her as thoughtfully. Holly needed to accept

that there would come a day she would no longer be haunted by a brief, albeit blinding four-day love affair, that left her wounded, broken-hearted and miserable. How long would her heart choose to belong to her Precious One ... the one who forgave her and wanted to marry her?

Holly's guilt flared sympathizing with Luka's plight. She secretly wondered if she could handle being around Kaine knowing there wasn't any future for them? Luka must have a strong faith.

What to do? She couldn't face him any longer knowing she brought him pain, disappointment, and an unimaginable torture.

After dinner, it would be time to leave. Her only hope was that the world she lived in at CMT-LA and Kaine's world in Europe, would stay apart. There should be little chance of collision when their worlds were in two separate orbits. Perhaps then, she and Luka would be lucky to find love together.

But there it was, every time she looked up into his cool blue eyes. The burning reminder — he was not Kaine.

By the time Holly stocked the dishwasher, she'd made up her mind, mistake or not.

"Luka, it would be best if you took me home tonight. This is so unfair to you." She shifted her weight to her other leg hoping he wouldn't argue with her. Or, try to convince her that she did belong to him, forever and always.

But he remained silent. Perhaps stunned, probably relieved.

"I don't know any other way to say this except to come out with it. After what has happened this morning, well, almost happened. I'll spit it out. Are you sure we can work so closely together with all these extenuating circumstances?"

Luka looked up and wiped his mouth with a cloth napkin demonstrating all the grace of an English gentleman. He struggled to hide the insult she had hurled his way. He delivered in an even tone.

"I'm a big chap, Babe." As he dropped the napkin on the table fixing his gaze on her to make his point.

He hadn't fooled her. She watched the painful expression as it grew on his face. She wasn't as convinced as his tone of voice set out to accomplish.

"I can handle my emotions. I'll never be the cause of your unhappiness. You've suffered enough."

She tipped her head in compliant agreement.

The drive to West Hollywood was quiet. Neither spoke, both lost in thought. He walked her to her door. She stood so close to Luka, she laid a hand on his soft, white cotton shirt. Her hand dropped to the waistband of his white baggy pant. She quickly pressed her lips to his smooth cheek kissing him lightly, below the bright red scar left by Kaine when he split Luka's skin. Possibly, she'd gotten to him and weakened him.

Instead, he managed a placating smile and announced.

"I'll see you at ten sharp."

"Perfect time to start a new life," she replied as cheery as possible.

"Luka, I want to thank you for everything you've done for me. If the timing weren't as it is, you would be the only one, and I'd run to you … you are my angel eyes." She lifted her hand and gently touched his freshly shaven cheek.

He took her hand in his.

"I know Babe, bloody rotten timing," he lamented punctuating his words with an acceptance that alarmed her.

She squeezed his hand tighter and tighter.

Luka Hunter stood for a moment until she surrendered to the ugly reminder that she'd let him go.

He waited patiently for his dismissal.

The embarrassment flushed her cheeks as she released her vice grip on him.

Luka didn't react. He quietly took his leave and skipped one step after the other up to the rear street entrance.

Holly held her raw emotions in check swearing to herself that she would not let him see that his rebuff crushed her spirit. She watched Luka's blonde silky hair, swaying back and forth on his shoulders with each step carrying him farther away from her, knowing she was a fool for letting Luka Hunter go.

Chapter Nine

YOU OUGHT TO KNOW

Holly huddled against the door jamb, trying to hide from the crushing despair of loneliness. There was no one to talk with because Allison, her best friend that lived upstairs, was in New York until after the holidays. She didn't have any close friends at the firm. At least not, close enough to discuss her raging dilemma between Kaine and Luka. Solange was busy being run ragged up north making wedding plans. Besides, Solange made it clear in London, her allegiance was to Kaine. And what of Emily? Kaine's sister. There was no need to enlist Emily as a friend; she was out of Holly's life.

The only high point of the solitude was that the media finally gave up and vacated the premises over the weekend. She was relieved another poor soul took center stage to be raked over the coals. She needed to remain old news and put the entire stinking ordeal of her as the Heart of the *Hurrikaine* far behind her. Even the photos in the European papers confirmed that Kaine entertained new lovers.

She needed to move on with her life.

Holly glanced at her message machine acknowledge the tiny flashing light. She robotically listened to the messages of unimportance, including another urgent one from Brett. Perhaps she would have lunch with him. She mindlessly fast-forwarded beyond Brett's predictable monolog until the last message. A soft British accent pierced her lonely world.

"Holly, it's Emily Jamison."

Holly instantly pictured Emily with her long, honey-blonde hair, big blue eyes, and lithe-framed body. She exhibited the similar Dunnehill family resemblance as Kaine, his only sister.

"I'm calling from Europe. I spoke to Solange and asked for your number. I hope it's all right to ring. I see you've popped out. I'll try to ring back later."

Holly was more than surprised Emily called at all. As wonderful as it was to hear Emily's friendly voice, it was one more reminder that Kaine was not far enough away. She busied herself, preparing her clothes for her first day at work as Luka Hunter's assistant, hoping to put Emily out of her thoughts. She didn't have pieces from the expensive Asset line to wear for Luka. Instead, she chose a tawny colored, tailored Yves Saint Laurent power suit with short sleeves, and two inches above the knee skirt because of the hot weather.

The phone rang.

Holly picked up the receiver on the first ring and cautiously answered hoping she'd not made a mistake by failing to screen it.

"Holly, Emily Jamison. I'm glad I've found you home. I've thought about you this past month and a half. How are you doing?"

"Better." She lied.

"It's good to hear from you. I'm surprised."

She had to ask, her curiosity was stronger than her pride. "How is ...he?"

"That's why I'm calling. Holly, my brother's miserable without you. He's refused to drop the last song "My Lady" from the set list. Yet it's sending him deeper and deeper into depression every time he sings it."

"I'm deeply sorry."

"I know. We all are. I wanted to call after I spoke to Solange because she explained you were upset about his moving on with his life. That you'd seen photos of my brother in the European papers with different women and that hurt you. Solange and I are hopeless romantics, and we're hoping you were upset because you care for my brother more than you want anyone to know.

"I wanted to be the one to tell you, the women are only fluff. He's not with any one of them for longer than a night if that. I think he's trying to prove to himself most of all he can go it alone without you. I believe he knows it's not working though I can't assure you he's not shagging any of them. He messed up on alcohol. I'd be surprised he could. Plus, there's Sarah to chase them off with a stick."

Stick?

A cold, hard gun was more to Sarah's taste, Holly thought.

"Nicky says the photos are good for publicity. But he doesn't understand how this type of publicity murders affairs of the heart."

It sounded to her like the affair in London was history for Kaine. He'd tried to give her a second chance, even a third, and a fourth but she'd rejected him each time. Emily's words weren't what she sought to hear.

"I appreciate your telling me, of course. He's parading about Europe with those foreign beauties hurt me terribly. It's been an extraordinarily low time realizing how quickly I was replaced in his life."

She took a breath and decided to reveal her current situation.

"News here is I've resigned from the law firm."

"That's bloody awful."

"Yeah, the sensational press coverage convinced my employer, I should take a long vacation. I was a mess for a few weeks, then my luck changed, and Luka offered me a job at CMT-LA."

"Luka? If he's in the picture. I'd call it bad luck."

"Don't do this Emily. I have to look forward to the challenge of becoming Luka's assistant."

"Assistant?"

Holly heard the sarcastic tone dripping in Emily's voice. And pushed to explain her point of view.

"It's that."

Holly unfolded the whole Malibu fiasco.

"You do see it was me. I wanted Luka. And though it may not sound like it, I do care for him. If I must confess the truth, a bit of me depends on Luka to remove the hurtful memories of your brother. Unfortunately, for Luka all his sincere efforts got him was pain. My love for your brother is too deep. It was Luka that stopped us from making love because I would have welcomed his tenderness and I would have made a terrible second mistake."

"Don't expect me to congratulate Luka for stopping. He was protecting himself, not your feelings." And as if adding, an afterthought asked. "Second mistake?"

"Yes, the first was allowing the Super Star to depart for Paris without me."

"You're so bloody right. What about Luka? How can you trust him? How can you let him convince you he will keep his distance? That doesn't sound like the Luka I grew up with — no not at all."

"Perhaps he's changed. Do you have any reasons why I shouldn't accept what he's promised?"

"I can list many. How long do you have?"

"Emily, please, I don't pretend to fathom your hostility toward Luka. Trust in my judgment. I won't encourage Luka. Have a little faith. Not all this pain is Luka's fault. If these were different circumstances, I would welcome a long-term relationship with Luka. I know he understands I am too much in love with your brother to make any commitment to him or anyone else. If by a miracle I ever get over Kaine Walker and Luka's around, I'd welcome him with open arms."

"Luka won't wait! You don't know him. He takes what he wants — when he wants it. If he's backed off, it's because he wants you to think that because he's cunning. And your every word frightens me more because I can hear the indoctrination, believing his lies. Let's not forget his incredible looks but phony charm. You can't trust him. Do you bloody well understand me? I was around Luka for the last decade and a half. And it's not because I'm Kaine's sister, but I want to see my brother happy with you. I wouldn't lie and make up hateful things about Luka to separate you. But I'm sorry, I know Luka Hunter too well, and I can't encourage *any* relationship with him. I'm thankful every day that he is out of our lives."

Holly remained silent, considering Emily's strong reaction to Luka. The reply seemed different from the usual envy, and Holly asked the obvious question.

"Has romance passed between you and Luka in the past, Emmy?"

No response.

Silence on the other end of the phone. Then the answer arrived swiftly.

"What happened in the past between Luka and me, I assure you is not the pressing issue."

Interesting, she didn't deny it. Luka and Emily had an affair. Something went sour, and she'd bet by the way Emily protested, Luka left her.

"It's the bad blood between Luka and Kaine that's important. You don't know about the constant competition between them. As far back as I can remember Luka's always needed to possess the women discarded by Kaine. And I don't mean to sound insensitive, but that includes you. I don't want to get into what went wrong with Luka and me. I'm sorry to be harsh, but you're in danger. Sometimes, I believe Luka became my brother's manager out of a desperate need to control Kaine."

"How can anyone control Kaine?"

"Luka can and does. Even fifteen thousand miles away, he's pulling Kaine's strings by being in L.A., with you."

That was what Luka said to Holly that fateful night at

Friar Manor after she confessed to Luka the engagement to Kaine, and then their plans to be married in Paris in three days. He'd said *if you make it to Paris.*

Emily made a few new points as Holly listened to the rest of her argument.

"Instead of being in Paris with Kaine, you're in L.A., with Luka. Kaine's no fool. He knows Luka better than any man on Earth does. He knows Luka *will* seduce you if he hasn't already by the way you are talking. That's what's tearing him apart. By your own admission, it almost happened today. It would have happened today if Luka wanted it. It wasn't in his plan. You don't know how clever he is. But I've always watched Luka, so jealous of Kaine. Yet, as Kaine's manager, he finally found a way to upstage him, to steal the spotlight from him. When it doesn't work, Luka goes after my brother's women. That's you. Kaine's always known, but Kaine didn't care until you. He's a fool like you. He loves Luka and would do anything for him. That is until today."

"Emily, are you sure? You make Luka sound so manipulative and malicious."

"Oh, I'm sure all right. Granted, Luka is a bloody good-looking man, but as the old cliché goes — so is Satan. Remember, he's the most beautiful angel tossed out of heaven. Next to my brother, well, you said it yourself. Kaine is the one, not Luka, Kaine! And I don't mean to sound as if I'm minimizing your skills and abilities, but this idea seems like another of Luka's master manipulations. You are the checkmate, stealing the Heart of the *Hurrikaine*. Picture the headlines?"

This was too much! Luka used her as a publicity stunt to

harass Kaine.

Holly needed to set Emily straight.

"Emily, Luka told me in London, that he isn't as interested in Kaine's women, as everyone said he was."

"Brilliant of him to bring it up first before one of us did."

"Luka's never shown any signs of wanting anything but the best for me. And it's all moot, anyway. Kaine doesn't want me. Not after the photos of him and the women. He is doing what he can to put London behind him as uncomfortable as that may be because he sees me with Luka. And the way I hate myself for my despicable betrayal I can't see facing Kaine again. And even if a way presented itself to see Kaine, I'm not sure what it would take me to apologize. I'm ashamed of my unacceptable behavior at Friar Manor. I'd never expect him to forgive me after that. Especially, after leaving with Luka. I can't see any future with Kaine. He hasn't tried to call or get in touch with me. No, Emily, your brother and I are finished. If there was a competition, it's finished."

"I wouldn't be so quick to say Kaine doesn't want you. Kaine is in love with you. Luka is obviously aware of that fact. If Kaine weren't battling the ghost of Briarwood, he would not be in this crippling depression. I can only hope once he overcomes this dark melancholy, he will summon his courage and go straightaway to L.A., for you. And Luka is counting on this. It will be the last confrontation. Honestly, I fear the outcome, whoever leaves this final round without you will surely perish."

"Emily you're so dramatic, I wouldn't have thought you capable of entertaining such histrionic delusions. I am *not* the grand prize!"

"I'll ignore your remarks, but if you don't heed my words, you'll learn the hard way. Luka knows Kaine better than Kaine knows himself. You are a *perfect* revenge. Most importantly, Luka knows victory is close. He understands that Kaine is fighting for his life. Every mention of you and Luka in the tabloids is like pouring boiling water on a gaping wound. I can't caution you enough.

"Beware of Luka's true motives, especially toward you. If you don't, you will be crushed by a darker side of Luka more frightening than any monster you thought my brother was down in the dark corridor at Friar Manor. With Kaine, he acted spontaneously because you betrayed him and his heart broke, causing him to lose his temper. With Luka, everything is premeditated and sinister."

Holly sat back and swallowed a sip of mineral water unable to take in this disturbing twist in the conversation. Kaine wanted her and loved her, after all, that happened. Luka was a monster with an agenda focused on her.

She scoffed, "Emily, Kaine is out of my life. And, I haven't anything to fear from Luka."

"You're not listening. Nevertheless, I do understand. Solange spoke the truth. Luka's brainwashed you. We hoped you'd listen to me. You're not, and you're not to blame. Luka is a master. He has you believing everything he wants. If you truly loved my brother, try to hear me.

"You're vulnerable. You haven't anyone to help you, but Luka. It's his way. He's planned it to isolate you. And after what you've dealt with, well, this call is long distance and repeating my warnings won't do any good. But I'll try one last time. Listen to me carefully. Watch yourself, but watch Luka even closer."

Holly didn't know how to explain to Emily the hold Luka had on her. But it wasn't an evil, sinister plan on his part. She exercised free will, but she was afraid to tell Emily that she was grateful for Luka, not wary of him. Emily was right, they were reaching a stalemate.

"You've been a good friend, Emily, to warn me and thank you for caring."

"I do Holly. I do. I hope no matter what happens we can stay friends though Luka will ultimately decide. I have to ring off and get back to Nicky."

"Say Hello, to everyone. I mean..." Holly decided to pause.

"I will," Emily replied.

After Holly had hung up, a raging river of swirling emotions pulled her down under a black cloak of depression. No distraction banished Emily's cryptic warnings from her mind. She picked up one of the newspapers with their love affair splattered across the front page.

Interesting, singing "My Lady" depresses him.

Why did he sing it?

Because Kaine was a businessman and his job was to sell love, their love. And if Emily was correct, it was an unbearable misery for him every time he went to work.

If she had it all to do over, she would have caught the Super Star, told Kaine about Sarah, and confessed the threat lodged against her. That she would shoot Holly with Kaine's gun and frame him for her murder.

Then immediately apologize to Kaine for her unspeakable betrayal with Luka at Friar Manor and begged for his forgiveness.

However, Emily's report on Kaine surrounded himself with new women did cause her to feel a secret victory that they hadn't erased her memory from him.

There was too much to mull over in her mind.

As her thoughts and emotions built up into an unmanageable tsunami, the moment arrived. She couldn't keep her head from falling back to allow the scream of loneliness and frustration to rip from her throat.

"K-A-I-N-E!"

Chapter Ten

BRINGING ON THE HEARTACHE

Time stopped somewhere between the dark edges of her thoughts. There in the shadows was where Holly hid. She lifted the bottle of Chardonnay to her lips. She planned to gather up her courage and face sleep, hoping she wouldn't find her dark-haired dream lover waiting. As day followed night, she endured another long, miserable night.

Holly awoke running for the toilet the next morning. She'd made a personal promise to stop drinking alcohol. It had to be contributing to this disruptive ritual each morning.

She lay wrapped in her comforter, planning her first morning at CMT-LA. Her trained, investigative mind, would not let go of her recent decision. This was the time to dig in and find out what the hell the ghost of Briarwood incident was about, that Emily thought important, as to mention it as a defense for Kaine? What happened long ago that it almost destroyed the man she loved?

After her stomach had settled, she primped. She stood blow-drying her hair straight, applied the office-appropriate makeup, quickly slipped into the Yves Saint Laurent, eggshell-colored, power miniskirt suit, and a black camisole. She looked around and then slipped into a black pair of heels and grabbed her black Prada bag after applying two sprays of Joy to her wrist. She hopped in her pride and joy, a restored forest-green 1977 MG MGB sports car and met Luka at CMT-LA.

It was an awkward reunion. Especially, after her embarrassing display at Malibu beach, coupled with Emily's scathing profile of the always handsome Luka. It was impossible to believe this man attractively dressed in a black Brooks Bros. shirt, new black 501 Levi's, and Gucci loafers, as sinister as the Prince of Darkness.

As if to show her nothing had changed between them, Luka took her hand in his. She was ashamed to admit how quickly his soft, smooth hand reminded her of their skills in Malibu. She swallowed a chunk of guilt, reminding herself, she was at CMT to work.

It took a few minutes to learn Luka was, as usual, commander-and-chief at CMT-LA. Impressed, but more puzzled, she wondered why he'd kept his distinguished position a secret? Why was every-fucking-thing about Luka Hunter a big secret?

For the first time since she'd met him, she entertained an objective thought — who was Luka Hunter? He shot to the top of her priority list to do a full profile.

The five-hour day sped by quickly, yet Holly was exhausted when she arrived home that night with her takeout dinner. She set a container of vegetable soup, chicken salad, and mineral water on the kitchen counter. Later she drifted to sleep, with the video of "Now That I've Found You" playing in the background like a ritualistic sacrifice to a dying religion.

Over the next three days, everything changed. By the end of the week, Holly relaxed, and enjoyed the challenges of various projects and especially working with Luka.

A man of many talents, she wondered why he believed she would keep all his secrets? At ground zero, he was teaching her the rudiments of the music business. Luka, a witty, lively, and informative teacher, never overwhelming her with too much information at a time. But she understood by his cherub smile that he was pleased she kept up with him. Then he'd taught her how to take directions from the early hours in London when he'd asked her to walk with him.

He would always reward her efforts with a flash of his sunny smile or a wink from his twinkling blue eyes. And when she was particularly attentive, a soft caress up the center of her back and always when no one around to see.

To her dismay, Luka kept up his business posture with her, and she found herself wanting to learn everything and have all of Luka. Then her world would be complete with all of his attention, to share his bed, his work, his dreams, and ultimately his life.

She wondered again.

Why did he believe in her?

After five short days, her life was filled with Luka. And it occurred to her this was the only way for him to keep her close, considering how jammed his schedule was. He had no time to babysit her. Was that why he was watching her? She hoped this wasn't a repeat of Brett, always keeping her close and involved to watch her.

Her legal training paid off making her able to grasp his

business ideas, proposals, acquisitions, and contracts promptly. And she was astute enough to see Luka was the mastermind behind CMT. Research produced a preliminary profile of him, and she learned that in little less than a year, he struggled to bring the ailing music channel from the brink of bankruptcy and changed it into a thriving competitor. CMT-LA was his baby and for some reason, he wasn't ready to share that information with her yet. She only knew he wanted her beside him.

Holly sat flipping through a stack of contract for his recent acquisitions to familiarize herself with the new areas CMT was breaking into around the world. Luka said there were no limits. It appeared he was right. She'd seen enough grooming at the law firm. She'd bet Luka was easing her into a prime spot, possibly as high as vice-something of CMT.

That wouldn't be the wrong career. She would spend all her days with Luka with the phone attached to his ear, delighted with each vicious deal of the day — and then all his sensual nights.

Every minute she was with him, drew her to him, closer and closer. She logged every possible hour, to be next to Luka to gaze into his expressive and intelligent, flashing blue eyes. Her admiration and respect grew for him. Before she knew it, Holly forgot about Kaine, Briarwood, and Emily with her harsh criticisms.

Her one focus, Luka.

On Friday, the last day of her first week of work she scheduled a follow-up doctor's appointment to get clearance to work full time. She glanced at her Bagheera watch, a gift from Brett, telling her it was close to time to leave. She looked up at

Luka, already missing him for the hour. But to lose an hour with Luka, anything might happen. She learned in five short days to thrive on the hectic pace when six overseas calls could be filling Luka's phone lines. In fact, so many companies sought Luka's consultations he hid more and more often in her tiny office. Luka sat behind her desk, his arms waving to make his point, arguing with an unsuspecting soul. She learned fast, those who crossed Luka, perished.

"It's business." He would say, shrugging his shoulders.

The tall stack of contracts she reviewed involved obscene amounts of money. Yes, Luka Hunter was the golden boy. Everything he touched turned to money. And she wondered if that would happen to her?

Holly glanced back down to the billion-dollar merger Luka was working on that week. She exhaled, thinking he was so young to be handling a colossal deal like this. He wouldn't give her all the details, but he'd said it would be his biggest acquisition. She caught a glimpse of his humility shine under the thick veneer of his English manners. How well he wore his power, his wealth.

Before Holly realized there was half-a-hour left, a tall, slim, black-haired beauty strutted into her office. She moved quickly to Luka sitting lost in paperwork at the desk. She moved close to him with an apparent familiarity.

The strange woman stood about five-nine. She was dressed in a top-of-the-line tailored, gray and white, pinstriped, Asset suit, that hung elegantly on her lithe frame. Her thick blue-black, shiny, hair hung long, and straight, to her waist. She carried the regal beauty of an old money Easterner. She had white, creamy, skin, intelligent, light-gray eyes, and perfectly sculptured nose only money could buy.

When the woman spoke, Holly was surprised by a slight, crisp, upper class, British accent, matching Luka's that flowed, giving her exact origin away.

"Here you are my luv. I've been looking everywhere for you. I've missed you at night," she spoke in an extremely sarcastic tone.

She closed the distance between them with confidence to stand at Luka's side. She placed an obligatory kiss on his cheek, leaving her lipstick branded on his skin.

Luka rose to his feet, but his taunt, facial expression said he didn't welcome the intruder. He took a step back as she flung herself on his chest, but his arms remained beside him.

She ignored his rebuff by seductively kissing him. This time, she aimed for those full, luscious lips, acting more like last night's lover than an uninvited intruder would.

A hot rush of jealousy scorched Holly's cheeks, thinking this woman might be how he spent his nights to satisfy his needs. Undoubtedly, Luka stashed women around the globe. But to see one come out of the woodwork unnerved her, to say the least. She remembered Claudine Michaels, the German supermodel, clinging to Luka in London with all the possessiveness of this woman standing before her did.

What was it about Luka that made a woman lose all her pride and self-control to own him?

But history reported one had been able to capture the magnetic Mr. Hunter's heart — Carrin — the woman she supposedly resembled. How had it happened that Carrin turned out to be a fool and left Luka for another man?

Holly hadn't been able to leave Luka for Kaine. Instead,

she'd left Kaine because of Luka. And, even though, the surprise of this forceful woman knocked Holly off balance, she suddenly realized what Emily meant about Luka. Her perceptions were twisted because Emily looked at Luka from the wrong perspective. Emily's loyalty made her misunderstand. She mistook Luka as a man taking Kaine's leftovers.

That might not be at all true. Perhaps Kaine was too difficult and unable to hold on to his spirited women. Holly was convinced that no woman in her right mind could deny Luka anything.

And Luka proved it once again to become the shining star, able to eclipse Kaine, the burnt out, crashing, rock star.

Could it be Kaine Walker's violent temper had been born out of his mounting jealousy of Luka?

Hadn't Kaine released his explosive rage on her in London?

Was that the prescribed punishment from Kaine when his women left him for Luka?

She shook her head. How far down the road of circumstantial evidence, she'd drifted — a rush to judgment for sure — convicting Kaine without hard evidence.

Holly stepped back and decided to observe this predatory woman. It became crucial to understand why women were compelled to choose Luka over Kaine. And more astonishingly, how she made his list of international beauties? He'd tried to explain it once. Something about her loving them for themselves, but that never satisfied her curiosity or answered what either saw in her?

Holly thought of the long, lingering looks the CMT

secretarial pool delivered as he passed. Or, any other women he passed by in the world, for that matter. The lithe woman on Luka's body wrapped herself around him. For the first time since she'd met Luka, he'd surrendered, by lowering his head and pressed his lips to hers. Any moment he would surely show this woman, her place. But Luka didn't stop. And like in London, when he kissed Claudine Michaels backstage, the maddening jealousy fired a blaze inside Holly.

Luka's arms relaxed and naturally circle the woman's back. It appeared he'd pulled her closer to him to prevent a thread from passing between them. The scene grew more intense for Holly. A moan of pleasure eased from the woman's mouth. Holly thought she would throw the stapler in her hand at them to break the provocative moment.

What the hell was Luka trying to prove?

"Ow," Luka yelled as he took a small step back.

He quickly grabbed the woman by the back of the head, pulling her head back by her hair and covered his lip with the other hand.

"You bitch." He hurled at her.

He twisted the long lock of hair another rung around his hand, forcing lines of an instant pain to spring on her face.

"I love your warm welcomes lover," she sneered, clenching her teeth.

Luka stepped forward, close to her, daring her to continue.

She held her ground.

Luka's face moved inches from hers. He released her quickly and took steps away from her.

And instead of moving away from him, the woman drew

closer to Luka, hovering on the side of him like a buzzing gnat.

Luka batted at her as if shooing away a pesky fly and continued to pour water and ice from a pitcher into a cup. He lifted a cube of ice to press against his lip.

She wore a fragrant Asset perfume, called Imagine that Holly couldn't afford with two weeks' pay,

The woman returned an icy glare at Luka, and her demeanor grew stiff and cold. Yet there was an unidentifiable display of strained emotion lurking below the perfected smile.

The sultry siren reached to assist Luka, but he pushed her off him with his hip.

She stepped back, shoving him gruffly away in return and caustically added.

"How was London?" She crossed her arms as she sat on the edge of the desk and crossed her long thin legs.

Interesting, this woman knew Luka from London. Holly was glad she was sitting down when the woman let loose with her next comment.

"Looks like Kaine got the bloody best of your arse again. Are you ever going to learn?"

Holly watched the woman lace her fingers in a long escaping lock of his golden hair that hung loosely over his shoulder, like a woman familiar with the best way his hair looked.

"How did you hear?" Luka scowled jumping to his defense.

"The tabloids silly." She twirled away like a child that carried a secret.

"You haven't heard? This is simply too delicious. Justice

served cold, at last. I'm finally in a position to bring you information on some nasty business all your paid assassins missed. Though how? It's inconceivable."

"What are you fucking going on about, Tess?"

"The tabloid headlines — the ones that read in bright red letters.

"Heart of the Hurrikaine A Mystery No More." She spoke slowly, using her hand to draw the sentence as an arc in the air.

"The pictures of Kaine's mystery lady, please, oh, but there's more. There's a photo of the schoolyard fight in London between the pair of you at Kaine's hotel. There are trashy of you and Kaine's tart naked! And, because I know you too well. I'm willing a large wager these pictures were either part of a business deal, a publicity stunt or..."

The venomous woman coyly placed a finger on her lip as if she'd guessed the secret. "... or ... your black heart decided it's payback time for Kaine?"

"Nude photos!!" Holly yelled out, as she shot to her feet from the chair with the force of a rising comet, making her presence known.

"Oh, I didn't know you were conducting a staff meeting?" The raven-haired beauty remarked, pointedly dismissing Holly.

Luka chided. "Well, finesse was never one of your strong points."

Rudely ignoring the woman, Luka turned to face Holly.

She noticed his bottom lip, puffy and rosy red in the center.

He spoke sarcastically through his teeth as if defeated.

"Holly, Contessa, Tessa, to all of her friends and loved ones."

Holly couldn't miss the added mockery in Luka's voice or the fact that he'd not explained his passionate response to this Contessa's possessive kiss.

"Tess, today is your lucky day. This is Holly Hill, Kaine's Mystery Lady."

"HA!!!" She scoffed. "She's no mystery any longer! Not after the world's seen the pair of you stark naked and fucking at the beach! Luka? Why do you always have to fuck all of Kaine's rejects? It's tacky!"

Holly was about to pop this rude and crude bitch right in her foul kisser when Luka spoke up to shut her up quickly.

"Why? You of all people should know," he mocked and wrapped a wry smile around the corners of his lips.

Everything was becoming twisted and distorted like a Fellini movie. Holly faced not only Kaine's ex-girlfriend but also Luka's. Did all women pass from one man to the other man as she had? Was she part of a pattern created by these internationally charming men? She wondered if she would ever escape their seductive web. Tessa obliviously hadn't.

What type of family was the *Hurrikaine* organization? Was it like the mob, no one got out?

Luka's voice rang out loud and angry charging into Holly's illuminating thoughts.

"You can cut the shit. You've made your point. But what's this about bloody nude photos?"

"Patience's pet, I want to savor every moment telling you."

Luka made a lunge for her.

"Oh, all right," she moaned reluctantly.

"You're certainly not as much fun anymore." She straightened her tailored suit jacket.

"The pair of you are baring it all at every checkout stand in America," Tessa boasted. Her eyes glittered, obviously thrilled to be the messenger with this juicy gossip. She licked her lips waiting for Luka to explode.

He did not disappoint her. "Which paper?" Luka shouted.

"All of them, luv, and every rag paper in the country, hopefully, the entire world. And you know in Europe, they don't have the protective black bars to cover your delicious gift." Tessa assured, glancing below his waist. Then her eyes swept over to encompass Holly. She lifted her eyebrows as if to seek Holly's critique of Luka.

Holly knew the woman presumed they were sleeping together. How disappointed Contessa would be to learn there was no such juicy gossip bonding their relationship. But then that was not Luka's fault was it? The filthy pictures would make everyone assume the same thing. She was sleeping with Luka. And then it hit her like a wooden plank behind her head.

Kaine!

To him, the photos would confirm any suspicions. And the photos would be what Emily described.

Boiling water poured on an open wound.

And there was something else she mentioned.

Luka will make you believe what he wants.

Holly shook her head, trying to clear her thoughts. She was becoming a certifiable paranoid.

Tessa leaned back and laughed in Luka's face, and then blurted, "There are no secrets left," and threw Holly a throw away glance as if to dismiss her.

Holly clenched her fist and took a step closer to Tessa.

Luka screamed for an intern. He sent him to the corner newsstand for the papers in question hollering to anyone nearby.

"Why wasn't I bloody told?"

Minutes later, under Tessa's abrasive stare, an uncomfortable, insecure Holly, peeked over Luka's shoulder. She stood riveted to the carpet in complete shock!

It was worse than she'd imagined.

There for the entire world to see, a full-page color photo. The photographer caught every disgusting angle, exposing Holly's nude body lying on her back. Luka's naked body draped half on hers, kissing her, his hands between her legs on the lounge chair, on the lanai.

There were others.

But the worst, the second incriminating photo of her on her knees in front of Luka before he'd helped her up from the sand. But the pause was when the photo was taken. It looked like what the photographer wanted — the lighting perfect from that angle.

The world would believe she was performing oral sex on Luka. They would accept that she was so sexually obsessed with him that she would submit to him not only in broad daylight but also in public. She shook her head, the captions under the photo read.

KAINE FINDS THIS HARD TO SWALLOW

The other photos were as compromising. The large, black,

inserted boxes served to draw more attention to her private areas, leaving little to the reader's imagination.

"Get me legal, this second!!!!" Luka screamed.

"I am LEGAL!" Holly whispered.

Luka corrected her. "Legal trained to fight these bastards? No! You can't take this on, you're trained in criminal law. CMT-LA retains a battery of entertainment lawyers paid big money to squash the fucker that took these offensive photos!" Luka bellowed.

Holly never saw Luka angry. Not even in London when he'd sworn to get even with Kaine for mistreating her. His face flushed with a bright red, and the vein in his forehead popped out, threatening to explode any second.

Holly took a breath and could scarcely summon the courage to turn the page. When she did, she discovered herself wrapped in Luka's arms topless, kissing him passionately on the sandy beach. More photos showed her stretched out alone, lying nude on the lounge chair sunbathing. The eye-catching black censored areas exposed all of her private moments to the world.

Holly turned away, placing her back to them knowing the humiliation spread quickly across her face. With each passing moment, it grew heavier until the weight of her despair forced her to lean against Luka's ridged body for strength.

What would her parents think?

What would Kaine think?

He wouldn't have the black bars.

Naked all over Europe!

And the knot twisted and tightened in her stomach. Holly was barely able to choke back the acidic bile following her anger. Then the utter despair washed over her brought on by this horrible violation. The sensational three-inch headlines read.

HEART OF THE HURRIKAINE EXPOSED
A MYSTERY NO MORE

Too incensed to catch her breath, Holly summoned the last of her control to focus and read the defiling article. It speculated on the details of her new position at CMT-LA, and her supposed blatant affair with Luka. They congratulated Luka for saving her from the decadent *Hurrikaine*. And more than hinted at how she'd landed the job.

"Luka, will I ever be free?" Holly spoke in a quiet, even toned voice that failed to hide her exploding anger. She vowed to hold her composure. Tessa would not witness her melt down into hysteria.

Luka entertained other ideas. He swiftly took Holly in his arms to comfort her.

Holly relaxed.

What if Tessa thought they were sleeping together? There were worse fates than people thinking this beautiful man was spending his nights with her — except for one, Kaine.

"Bloody hell, Luka, is this necessary?" Tessa briskly protested.

"Isn't this how you two got into this mess? I mean before you became headline news?" And she laughed again in a loud and disgusted tone.

Tessa's laughter became louder and louder filling Holly's ears. For moments, Holly pictured everyone laughing at her.

She wanted to cover her ears as she hid her face in Luka's chest.

Then the cold, unrelenting Tessa continued to speak.

"I don't see what the big deal is? What makes her special Luka? Or?"

Right on cue, the obvious observation. "Is it? She bears an uncanny resemblance to Carrin. Believe me. She's no Carrin."

Luka exploded. "Tessa, that's it! OUT! Maybe, you should learn to watch your fucking mouth! Get the bloody hell away from me!"

Then as quickly as he flared up, he cooled and calmly asked, "Are you staying at the marina on the boat?"

Tessa smiled. She'd taken no offense at Luka's harsh outburst and sweetly replied. "Where else, my darling, it's the only decent thing I've ever gotten from you."

Luka shot Tessa, another spine-chilling look.

Tessa shook it off like raindrops. Then she looked to Holly advising.

"Holly, if I were you, I'd stick with Kaine. He's a much better lover than Luka. Don't you agree?"

Luka's response was predictable. He stepped away from Holly and screamed.

"That's it bitch! Get the fuck out!"

Tessa's smile grew full with satisfaction, pleased she'd pushed the right button. Unruffled by Luka's outburst, and the galling pleasure stamped on her face that she won this round with Luka, Tessa gracefully gathered her Asset clutch, blew Luka an affectionate kiss and admitted.

"I've always loved you most when your veins bulged."

She left the innuendo hanging in the air a moment, then

added.

"Call me soon. I'm in town — for a while."

And like the noxious whirlwind she was the Contessa vanished.

Luka was livid, unable to conceal his upset. His beautiful face flushed a bright red, his breath becoming sharp and labored.

Holly knew he was too much of a control freak to accept being caught off balance.

His fist hit the desk with a loud thud. "That fucking bitch. She loves to stick it to me."

"Who *IS* she? I assumed by her tasteless remarks she was once a girlfriend of Kaine's? And yours?" She speculated, hoping to soothe Luka and not enrage him.

Holly took a step closer to him, drinking in his mint-scented breath and reached for a tissue to wipe the mark of Tessa from his lips. She'd remembered another time backstage in London she'd had to clean another woman's lipstick off the irresistible Luka Hunter.

He changed his position causing his head to move away from her as if he didn't want to talk about it.

But he did.

"Kaine was a momentary acquisition of hers. He was bloody lucky, it was short and deadly. I wasn't so lucky."

"Why? Who is Tessa to you?"

"Let's say, if anything questionable ever happened to Tessa, I'd be the number one suspect. She's trying to eat me alive like a fucking Black Widow spider!"

Chapter Eleven

FOUND OUT ABOUT YOU

Holly understood the warning look on Luka's face — don't ask — don't ever ask.

But that wasn't Holly's nature.

She responded cautiously.

"Luka, Black Widows eats their mates!"

"Yes, Holly. You're bloody right. Tessa's my wife..."

Whatever she anticipated, those were not the four words. Holly choked on a breath and barely exclaimed.

"What? You didn't say."

"Yes, I did. You heard me correctly, my wife."

Her knees dissolved to liquid and looked around for a chair to catch her limp body. As she sank into it, she dropped her head into her hands.

He added quickly. "But we're separated."

She looked up to see how the lines of concern etched across his beautiful face.

"I can't understand why you didn't tell me you were married before you ever kissed me in London or why no one told me?"

"It's not a secret. I would assume everyone thought you were aware or because it's not a big deal. Tess and I are separated, about four years. I've started divorce preceding's a number of times. Then I'd drop it. This will be like any expensive Hollywood divorce and kill me — financially. I haven't spent these last fifteen years building a global empire to give any of it to her. I'd rather see her dead."

Holly's face must have turned ashen, because Luka smiled one of his bright, sunny smiles to warm her, to put her at ease after his threatening comments. I hadn't worked.

"I meant figuratively, of course. I've been waiting and hoping she'll fuck up for leverage in court and secure a reasonable settlement. But these photos of me naked bum with you could give her all the ammunition she needs to put the screws to me."

Luka threw himself into the desk chair.

But Holly reeled from the fact that Luka was married.

"When is everyone going to understand that I didn't come with the *Hurrikaine* encyclopedia of knowledge and facts?" She watched him realizing that the revelation of his marriage would come with ramifications.

"Fuck," he snarled as he rested his forehead in his hands, his fingertips rubbing his temples. Then he pulled a handful of hair through his fingers.

"Unfortunately, your disappointment over my legal unavailability isn't currently my biggest problem. The European newspapers have been carrying stories about her involvement with a wealthy, shipping magnate who intended to marry her. But she's a cunning bitch, and she wants her own money or should I say, MY MONEY!!! And these photos may mean she'll collect."

Holly moved out of the chair, walked up close and bent near his face. She pressed a quick kiss to his cheek, hoping to soothe his frayed nerves. She took another tissue and started once again to clean the red lipstick mark from his face while trying to understand. She spoke of her shattered feelings to him with surprising ease.

"These past few months have been a difficult time for me. It seems every day something earth-shaking happens to me. I'm more confused than ever. You're married meaning we have no future until you're divorced. So what was supposed to be going on between you and me in London and in Malibu?"

Luka pulled her down on his lap. His hand slipped around her head and pulled her face close, oh so close.

"Babe, nothing — Kaine, Tessa, these photos, — I repeat, nothing's changed my feelings about you."

Luka pressed his warm, moist lips against hers, with more restrained passion than she wanted to admit. Luka's kiss was powerful, alerting every cell in her body. She understood why he was going to give her the time she needed, not only because he loved her … but because he needed time to clean up his own mess.

Luka gently lets her go as she groped for a refreshing breath. She understood then, whether she liked it or not, Luka would have to be dealt with soon, very, very, soon.

Luka looked deeply into her eyes, brushed his lips across her cheek, and reminded her.

"It's as I've told you. I've cared for you since the first time you fell into my arms on the street in Chelsea. It bloody well nearly killed me to hand you over to that bastard Kaine. But by then you saw stars. I knew we couldn't start a real relationship until you purged Kaine from your system. I misjudged you thinking it would take you long to find out about him.

"I have a lot of baggage to clean up with Tessa. And after what happened between the two of you at Friar Manor, I accepted the fact that he may have destroyed your trust in yourself. Then I'd never have a chance with you. As for Tessa, believe me. I never expected Tessa to blow into town today. She'd been out of my life and living in Europe for the last three years. Undoubtedly, it was the smell of making money from the tour that appealed to her."

Luka's kiss derailed her clear thinking more than she would have liked to admit. But her curiosity returned. Thoughts spinning, she needed answers to this new mystery and exactly where she fit in his life.

"How long have you been married?"

"Seems like bloody forever ... close to eight years. I knew Tessa before the band. And she is part of the early history of *Hurrikaine*." Luka briefly explained.

This could be a break, she thought. Though Tessa was extremely unpleasant, she may be able to shed important insights about Briarwood. That is if she knew what was going on there before the band's inception. She could only hope Tessa would become a solid lead.

"Tessa and I were together for a while. Later it was her and Kaine when the band was playing pubs in London. Things fell apart between them because of Kaine's violent attack on her. I was there for her again. Then other bloody awful things happened to keep us together, and well, eventually we married."

A few things became clearer. Kaine and Emily's warnings confirmed there was a strange history between the two men. And here was Luka cleaning up after Kaine — again. She was starting to picture herself as the pawn, in an elaborate game between these two formidable men. A destructive game being played out internationally.

Holly's internal alarm system screamed.

Run for your life!

Her hand went to her waist, nauseous again.

And that's when the revelation hit her.

Are you Luka's whore?

Holly remembered Kaine screaming at her at the castle and in the corridor at Friar Manor hurdling the angry reference at her. She understood because Luka was married. And he'd believed, like everyone else that she'd known. But she hadn't. And if she had, she would never lit the match to play with fire. Her head spun, and her body was woozy. She needed to do something.

"Luka, my nerves are shot. I have to be at Dr. Cooper's in exactly two minutes, then go home and rest. I'm too dizzy to drive, please find someone to take me, and then have them drop my car at home?"

"I'll drive you, Babe. I need fresh air too." He suggested flatly. He forced a smile and wrapped his arms loosely around her waist, then hit a button on the intercom. After he'd left instructions for the battery of CMT-LA lawyers to suck out every drop of blood from the tabloids and photographers and for someone to drive Holly's car home, he cleared his afternoon meetings. Half an hour later, he pulled off Wilshire

Blvd., into the doctor's underground parking structure in Beverly Hills.

Holly and Luka sat patiently waiting for the lab to return the blood test results. The doctor searched for a reason why she was so exhausted and nauseous. But after the roller coaster life, she'd led, what did she expect?

Secretly, Holly worried it had something to do with the cocaine she'd done with Kaine in London, for three high-flying days. She didn't understand drug cycles and with all the press about addiction, she was nervous. Could these symptoms be side effects or withdrawal?

It didn't help when the doctor called her into his private, affluent office. His face was solemn. Holly slipped her trembling hand into Luka's strong, steady hand. She pulled him near her for emotional support as they sat side-by-side. Luka squeezed her hand tightly as the doctor spoke, and Holly thought he would have made a perfect poker player.

"I have good news. Your ribs are healed as expected. The cocaine abuse wasn't substantial, so nothing to worry about there. That's not creating your present symptoms. But the blows to your head, initiating the concussion, could be residual effects causing your dizzy spells. But the nausea is a symptom. Congratulations, judging by your test results, you are seven weeks pregnant."

"Pregnant?" The word pierced her heart like a jagged knife, one rung at a time.

"Dr. Cooper, how can this be?" The words popped out before she could swallow them.

"Holly, I'm sure I don't need to explain how this works?" He imparted with a fatherly tone, showering her with a large, warm smile then winked at Luka, for a job well done.

Holly forced a smile as she settled back to lean into Luka's waiting arms, pulling her to his chest.

She sat dumbstruck.

Never. Never, had she imagined she was pregnant.

Pregnant?

But the signs were there. Some detective she was. The awful morning sickness should have tipped her off at some point. What about the constant tiredness?

Yet in those moments, she was devoid of any emotions. Luka's warm support flowed into her from his comforting embrace as he squeezed her, accepting the doctor's diagnosis, giving her the necessary strength to realize what happened to her.

Luka took over after a long, uncomfortable silence.

"I'm sure I don't need to remind you how highly confidential this meeting has become? Tabloids especially. We'll take it from here. We'll be in touch soon for instructions. We need to go somewhere private straightaway and talk."

The doctor smiled in agreement.

If the tabloids got a hold of this, she thought.

Luka, as usual, was cool, calm, his mind racing, already far ahead of her. She wondered how he did it. Luka stood and respectfully shook the doctor's hand and escorted a dazed and worried Holly out the door.

"I'm taking you to that Italian restaurant in the canyon. We can talk there without any press to bother us. We can't allow them to get a hold of this news." He didn't need to finish his sentence.

For once, he wasn't that far ahead of her. She saw the

headline.

HEIR TO *HURRIKAINE* FORTUNE

Luka continued. "Since the beach photos have made us a headline in the tabloids, I'll assume your place will be surrounded by media."

Holly tipped her head as if she'd heard him.

When?

When? Was all she could think?

Holly didn't see any of the West Hollywood landscape. She never heard the songs, pouring from the radio or the wind whipping her hair about her face. She didn't notice anything.

When did it happen?

Luka parked on the tiny street behind the canyon store. Then he came around to open her door.

Holly sat motionless for a moment. She looked up into Luka's beautiful eyes filled with pain and worry over her.

She reached out to take his hand, bearing her pain and anguish.

"What am I going to do? I have Kaine's baby growing inside of me!"

Chapter Twelve

DAZED AND CONFUSED

Holly sat with Luka in silence. She pushed the pasta around her plate with a fork. It was impossible to accept this shattering news.

Luka married.

Seven weeks pregnant!

When could it have happened? The preposterous idea absorbed her every thought. She quickly inventoried her entire London affair with Kaine, and that Luka's insufferable patience had kept them apart. As complicated, as the state of affairs between them was becoming, at least, she didn't have to wonder which lover was the father. Oh, the horror of that!

This baby was unmistakably Kaine Walker's. She scoured each encounter with Kaine. She distinctly remembered their jokes about protection, his satchel with the foils and her colorful lollipop condom collection. Over and over, she ran the scenarios of their lovemaking until she ferreted out the only possible occurrence. Other than a defective condom, the one moment there'd been no time — when Kaine returned from the sound check.

Their child conceived then!

The only possible time.

Luka pressed. "What Holly? Tell me what you are thinking. Your face! Please don't lock me out."

Holly shook her head no.

"It couldn't be." She protested under her breath.

"I remember when it happened, Luka." She poured out the whole story when Kaine returned to the suite drunk on whiskey, high on cocaine. The words tumbled out gradually, details of Kaine's forceful treatment and neither of them remembering the protection.

"I knew something bloody well happened that day. Why didn't you let me take you from him, then?"

"Because he'd apologized," she clarified in a tone of she'd made a mistake, and pulled the napkin up to catch her falling tears.

She quietly added, "And like a fool, I believed him. He didn't hurt me, more like scared me, with his explosive passion. But the fruit of that time with him ... to have conceived our child in such a manner distresses me."

Holly leaned back and sighed in a disgusting tone.

Luka reached over and covered her hand, his eyes gentle, but laced with a sternness she'd never seen. She knew whatever was coming would require all of her attention.

"Holly, no one knows better than me how complicated my life is, and I give you my word, I'm filing for divorce as soon as it can be arranged. Until then, I'll stand by you. If you want this baby. I'll stay if you want me. If you don't want the baby, I can make arrangements."

There was, at least, one thing Holly knew for sure.

"Oh, no Luka, I couldn't do anything to harm my baby. Kaine's baby."

With that admission, Luka became incredibly irritated. This final piece of news seemed to push him to the edge of his usual composure. It hadn't been a good day for him either Tessa, naked photos, and a baby.

"Blast Kaine! Are you saying you're going to stand behind him? Holly wake up, please! I know that Kaine does love you, but don't you see that with the baby, you have to think of yourself! And if not yourself, then think of your baby's future. How good is it to have a rock star, vagabond for a father?"

Holly knew Luka was spot on and accepted she could never hope for a normal life.

Kaine had been right too.

You have no idea what you are getting into.

This was awful. She couldn't control her pent-up tears as they dripped down her cheeks.

"I know Luka, and I can't think about that. Please, try to understand. I have to get used to this news. After the press, the beach house, those horrible photos, you, Tessa, how much can I take?

"I'm not used to my life moving fast. I can't believe how mellow my life was. Even the Collins murder trial, with all the twists, turns, and international coverage that was mellow compared to the last couple of months of my life! I never know what's going to happen." She'd divulged quickly and sipped at her mineral water to steady her cracking voice.

"Since winning the CMT contest, I've been thrown into a turbulent and unpredictable world that I never knew existed.

I've had enough new experiences to last me a lifetime."

Holly lowered her eyes to follow the napkin she twisted about one finger, sorry to unload on Luka, and she dropped her head. What she didn't say, the man she loved more dearly than life itself left her with an incredible gift, a piece of him growing inside of her. The one thing he wanted the most, his dream come true — to make a baby with her. She looked up to Luka and forced a sympathetic smile.

"I understand this situation is not fair to you, standing by me like you have. But I have to think about this Luka and for a long while."

Luka hung his head in despair and then ran his fingers through his long hair. He sat back, straightened his spine, and took a long swig of his mineral water.

"Remember Babe, you're the one that didn't get on that plane in London with him." His words hung heavy in the air then added.

"You're right, of course. I agree you need time to work out a suitable outcome for this situation. I caution you. Don't take too long. Your condition has an expiration date. The babies' growing every day and you have a few precious weeks to decide how you want to announce this pregnancy to the world."

Her heart wrenched, straining the bond of her abiding love, prompting a deep need to defend Kaine.

None of what Luka said was true. And none of this would have happened if she'd listened to Kaine and stayed out of Luka's way.

But she didn't speak her thoughts aloud. Yes, she quite agreed, she didn't get on the plane. But not for the reasons

Luka believed. She'd loved Kaine — always would.

Holly thought of Kaine's brilliant love, his generosity, kindness, and gentleness with her. When she'd basked in Kaine's pure love, they'd been the finest moments of her life. He had been warm and loving, even after betraying him, he'd forgiven her. And one thing she knew for sure, he would want this child.

Holly reached for her glass, her hand shaking. She couldn't tell Luka, she couldn't hurt him. Instead, her tears of frustration burst forth as she grabbed her purse and jacket and then hurried outside to Luka's car.

He joined her moments later.

"Take me home, please. I need to be home."

"What about the press? They'll expect a statement about the photos."

"We'll deal with them like we do everything, Luka. Together."

"That's my girl. I told you, you're stronger than you think."

He was right.

Luka drove up the canyon road to Holly's street. Vans lined the winding road long before they approached her place. Luka fought back the press at her gate as he led Holly beyond the barrage of unanswered questions. And when inside, they were relieved the press kept a respectable distance.

But that was all that was going her way.

"Babe, I've got an important meeting this evening. I'm sorry. I can stay with you for the time being. Remember, you won't have to be alone in any of these." Luka crossed the floor in three strides, took her in his arms, and pressed his lips to hers ever so gently.

She couldn't respond. It was as if she cheated on Kaine, all over again.

Luka pulled away and stepped back, his eyes said he understood. But the kiss said otherwise. The whole situation was so unfair.

"Think about this while I'm gone. I'll stand by you. We can announce this baby as my child. No pressure, only if you want. After all this recent press, it wouldn't be hard to convince anyone. It could work Babe, think about it."

"LUKA HUNTER!!!! That's the most unselfish suggestion I've ever heard." She remarked, genuinely astonished. Was there no end to the sacrifices Luka would endure for her?

"You would do that for me?"

"I will continue to tell you until you believe me. I'm not Kaine. I'd do anything for you."

She stepped closer to Luka, oh so close. She rested her hands on his soft shirt. His heart beat beneath like a hummingbird. She wanted to throw herself into those arms that held her and comforted her too many times. But this situation was not fair to Luka, always strong, always loving.

"Considering your tempestuous history with Kaine, you would do this for me? Give my, or I should say, our baby, your name?"

"If that's what it takes to make you happy. Yes, I will in a minute, Babe."

Holly was astonished because she'd never been the recipient of such devotion. And taking another step closer, she pushed her body into his and wrapped her leg about his. She slid her arms around his shoulders and up Luka's long, sleek neck. She paused and looked into the eyes of a beautiful man. His eyes said he loved her. And she wondered if she would ever hear those words again from him, though every day, Luka showed her in a million ways.

She tiptoed up to kiss him, long and meaningful, then pulled away, yet remained in the warmth of his strong arms and confessed in a quiet and remorseful tone. "I don't have any answers. I need to think."

"Of course," he agreed.

Luka Hunter, a most extraordinary and patient man, hugged her and left.

Volcanic thoughts swam in her head.

Kaine's BABY!!

Amazing but true.

Her motherly hands instinctively went to cover her lower abdomen — nausea and fatigue, a baby, a baby Kaine. She pictured Kaine's long, dark hair on the infant, with his large Technicolor blue eyes. Her young son-to-be, of course, a son, Storm, was what Kaine wanted to name him. Storm it was. But if not male, then this baby was Savannah. Kaine's choice of name for his daughter.

Holly flipped on her TV, and she absent-mindedly clicked the remote. That is until she stopped when the dial hit CMT. It was running a black and white reel of a dark, misty room. Fresh, stinging tears glazed her eyes as she watched the camera holding a close up of her face. A shot of Kaine gradually would follow. Then the camera moved back to her while the wind blew long wisps of her hair across her face.

Holly jumped up and threw in a fresh videotape and

pressed record hoping to capture more of the beginning. As their video continued to play, she folded her legs up around her chest. Her body stiffened, and she gnawed on her bottom lips as she waited, anticipating Kaine's life-altering kiss. She saw the shadow approaching. She saw him coming for her, then behind her. Her tears of loss and pain lined her cheeks.

How awful.

She loved her man named Kaine. On and on she watched, witnessing the passion in his eyes for her the first moment he saw her face. And then he'd kissed her.

Her reliving the experience twisted her insides, and her sobs grew louder. And as if saying the words aloud would be magical, she whispered.

"I can't lose this baby, not Kaine's baby."

The video played itself out. And as she imagined the castle scene, fit beautifully. She wondered what Kaine's final thoughts were on the video were since he'd little involvement with postproduction because he'd left that to Luka.

Did his heart break like hers did, watching it over, and over again?

How did he react watching them together?

Did he see the same magic and chemistry they had shared between them?

Did he remember how their love was special?

Like no other, he had once said.

"Now That I've Found You" surely a guaranteed hit would constantly replay on CMT. That would unquestionably be added to her torture, hearing it played all over L.A. She knew she would not be strong enough to ignore the video. It would be another torment, able to view her in his arms anytime she wanted. This was too much information to process.

The list for the day was staggering. Too much happened.

Would she tell Kaine of his child? And if so when and where?

Then there was the Briarwood mystery.

Of course, the pressing question — who was Luka Hunter — TRULY!

And how married was he?

Who was Carrin that she resembled? And why was no one talking about her?

Was Carrin a secret like Tessa?

Why had no one mentioned the small fact that Luka was married?

How did Tessa fit into the tightly fitted puzzle?

And what was that remark about Kaine's violent attack on Tessa long ago?

And the baby. Why was Luka willing to become her child's father?

Why? Why?

Too many questions.

No answers.

For the moment, all the distressing questions needed to be put to rest. Holly knew there was only one place in the world she wanted to be where she felt safe and comfortable. And that was tucked away in Kaine's loving arms. Given the opportunity, she vowed, she would make certain she'd never leave Kaine again.

Then the overwhelming sadness settled into her soul when the concert part ran on the screen. She could barely watch Kaine. The shots of him singing in Paris, with his hand wrapped in a cast, his spirit broken, shattered her heart once again. He didn't look good, in spite of the heavy stage makeup. His eyes showed his tired and drawn spirit.

His sparkle dead.

As Emily described, h*e is miserable*. When the video ended, she picked up the remote, rewound the tape to watch again. She thought about the timing of the release of their video and the news of their expected child colliding at the same time. And she knew in her deep, private, heart-of-hearts, that she would never be free of Kaine Walker, Duke of Briarwood, the father of her child, even if she never laid eyes on him again.

Chapter Thirteen

THE WAY WE WERE

How long Holly sat lost in the magic of the music video was uncertain. She wrapped the comforter tightly around her legs and pushed her arms inside the sleeves of her *Hurrikaine* jacket. She breathed in his scent, remembering how he'd given it to her at Briarwood Castle.

Holly replayed her moments with Kaine with a fever that bordered on manic. The longing for him kept bringing her to tears. It was as if everything froze in time as long as the video played. She relived those sweet moments with him as if they would never end. How accurate the lyrics of the song that lured her to Kaine had become, "Now That I've Found You."

Holly sat on the edge of the dark shadows and sipped her mineral water. She needed to take good care of herself. Nothing could jeopardize this pregnancy. She wouldn't, it was that simple. After all, she'd been through she couldn't possibly lose this baby.

She grabbed a ragged breath and her hand instinctively moved to rest over her abdomen. Dr. Cooper didn't entertain any detrimental ideas that her recreational drinking and drugs with Kaine in London had been enough to cause any permanent damage to the developing fetus.

Holly rushed along the steady current of memories, back to pleasant times with Kaine, the scent of him and all the times they made beautiful love in his castle, his home. She remembered the fire in his touch and his gentle, loving caress. And a tiny smile curled at the edge of her lips, remembering the many sweet times in his suite when they unknowingly been a family. Maybe the only time they would be a family under one roof.

She looked out the window. The sky grew darker. How late was it? She didn't know, didn't care. She hadn't heard anything from the reporters camped outside the gate. She didn't dare peek out there. She'd become like Kaine, a prisoner of her own doing once again.

Holly broke the self-induced trance to heat chicken soup while the ring of her phone followed her into the kitchen.

She ignored the caller until she heard the soft British accent.

Chapter Fourteen

STOP DRAGGING MY HEART AROUND

H olly gushed with happiness as she welcomed the familiar voice.

"Emily?"

She knew she would hear news of Kaine.

"It's good to hear your voice." Perfect timing.

"Are you doing better Holly?"

"Yes, I saw the doctor. I've been given a clean bill of health." Holly waited for Emily to respond. Instead, she was quiet.

Something was wrong.

Emily was too quiet.

A serious tone laced Emily's well-chosen words when she started to speak.

"I don't know if you are aware, but unflattering pictures, to say the least, about you and Luka, are splashed on every newsstand across Europe? And I'm not sure you remember? Over here, they don't use the black censor boxes the States papers require."

Emily's voice rose to a high pitch, almost to a shrill exposed her upset by the publicity.

Her words came hard and fast. "I'm thankful we'd spoken before the newspapers hit the streets, Holly, they're shocking and incriminating. I need to tell Kaine the truth about you and Luka at the beach. Please, before he sees the papers if he hasn't already. He's rapidly slipping into a deep, destructive, depression. The band fears he won't be able to continue the tour. Holly, what do you think I should do?"

Before Holly thought her answer through, she blurted.

"Why the hell should he care what I do? Or, whom I do it with, Emily? Kaine Walker made it clear he has a new life. Don't I have the right to start a new life too?"

Her own harsh words surprised her, considering her loving, reflective thoughts minutes ago. And when she sought another breath, the remorse flowed in by the buckets crushing her heart.

Holly's soul cried out to comfort her lover's pain, remembering it had been a careless moment kissing Luka at Friar Manor that started this battering of destruction. She knew of no way to squelch the anguish she'd brought to Kaine's family and friends.

She grabbed a ragged breath and tried to find the words to reassure Emily the best she could.

"I'm sorry you're dragged into this mess. I never wanted this. I wish things could have turned out differently. Then there would be no photos to explain. I hate to admit, as much as I hurt Kaine in London, I miss your brother constantly, and it never stops hurting."

Holly fell silent, thinking about her baby as her hand went to cover her stomach.

It hurts so much, bounced in her mind.

"But for selfish reasons, I can't explain, I can't let you intervene."

Emily remained silent.

In the silence, Holly sought to smooth over the shock of the demoralizing photos.

"Please, Emily. Do you think he will hate me forever?"

"I can't tell you what Kaine's planning. He won't talk to anyone. I'm hoping he'll remember how the press has treated him abominably over the years, and he'll realize he shouldn't believe what he sees or reads. But Holly, the photos, if I hadn't heard your story first from you, I confess, it would be impossible to rationalize them away.

"If Kaine's seen them, you can imagine what nightmares he is fighting. Holly please, I implore you to let me TELL him. It's not a secret between you and me that he loves you. But there's a good reason to justify why he's staying away. It's killing him, I know that much, especially to see you with Luka. That's an unforgivable betrayal to him. He keeps threatening to kill him."

Holly hung her head low, allowing the power of the shame to pour over her. The horrid turns in events never seemed to stop. The guilt stabbed at her stomach. But it wasn't a situation in which she'd any control. But that rationalization did nothing to stop the demons dancing in her stomach, causing her a miserable pain. It was time to own up about Malibu. She took a deep breath of courage and told the truth.

"That's another major problem, Emily. In truth, I almost

made those disgusting photos come true. Listen, not all of this fiasco is Luka's fault. Believe me, when I say I was alone and too ashamed to face Kaine after Friar Manor. It looked to Kaine like I brutally walked out on him. If only, well, it did happen. Luka was nothing short of a blessing. He's been incredibly supportive during each turbulent upset."

Emily's tone rose sharply.

"Perhaps too supportive, Holly. I don't buy his rescue act. I know it's essential for you to secure a job. But I suggest that you keep a reasonable distance from Luka if you entertain any hopes of ever reconciling with my brother. There's bad blood between them these days."

Silence passed along the line. Holly sat thinking about the baby that shared her body, her actual blood, mixing with Kaine's blood … the blood of the *Hurrikaine*.

Emily choked back a cough and broke the silence, clearing her throat.

"I have good news, Holly. I hope you can share this special news with me, in the light that it's intended."

"I need good news."

"I'm going to have a baby," Emily spoke. The exact words perched on the tip of Holly's tongue.

The synchronicity dumfounded Holly.

"Oh, Emily, I'm sincerely happy for you and Nicky, warm and happy congratulations."

This was excellent news. Emily would be with Nicky, her husband and lead guitar player for *Hurrikaine*. She would be with the man she loved and together they would raise their child in a home full of love.

Holly drifted for a moment to the scene the last morning

at the airport in London.

If I'd only gotten on THAT DAMN PLANE.

But she hadn't.

This would have been a joyous time for sister and brother, both about to become parents.

Emily broke into Holly's train of thought.

"Thank you, Holly. You're the second person I've shared this news with and, of course, Nicky thinks all is brilliant. The sad part is keeping the news from Kaine, but he has enough to deal with at the moment."

The pangs of guilt tighten again in Holly's chest, sending quick, sharp pains to pierce her broken heart.

"Yes, I'm so sorry he does. But why keep this good news from him? I would think his becoming an uncle would cheer him up immensely."

"It's a trying story. Nicky and I have attempted to start a family for years. It's been very hard because historically I miscarry in the first trimester."

Holly had the first-hand experience of the devastating disappointment associated with the word miscarry, and her heart went out to her friend.

"My depression after each of these has contributed to most of our rocky marital problems. And Kaine, he always worries when I'm pregnant. He'll be a smashing father."

Holly wasn't surprised, she'd known.

"I don't want to worry him needlessly unless unavoidable. It's been four months and my specialist believes I'm out of harm's way."

The news of Emily's baby was almost too much for Holly as she sat weighing the pros and cons of sharing her own explosive news with Emily.

Emily continued, "That's why I went on holiday, to a remote village in Spain, to rest and keep my baby. All the pressure of the band recording and getting ready for their first tour in four years took a toll and more stressful than the specialist wanted me to handle.

"Nicky's been involved from the early planning stages, and it took him away from me for days on end. Nicky and I were fighting a significant amount of the time he was home. I couldn't bring myself to tell Nicky and worry him with an additional burden. With Luka leaving the management of the band up to him and Kaine, they are handling and making the arrangements. They both have become extraordinary businessmen."

No doubt, Holly thought, with Luka as a teacher.

"I told everyone I needed to get away for a while alone, although my leaving upset Nicky more than I ever imagined. I never thought he'd miss me being away as much as he had since he was in meetings day and night. But he did, and all is forgiven because he knows why I had to leave him.

"Can you hear what I'm saying? Sometimes, people who love you the most, have to leave. Perhaps my brother is a bit like me. He needs to get away to finish or start something important. Something that is so important, your whole future is riding on it. We can only hope the end will turn out as it has for us.

"I'm home, we are more in love than ever, and he fusses about me like an old mother hen. Life's hard on Nicky these days, but he wouldn't have it any other way. He's forced to make time to handle most of the business after Luka's departure and while Kaine is unable to contribute.

"It's odd, my leaving to preserve my marriage, almost cost me my marriage and then gave me my marriage back stronger than ever." Emily stopped speaking.

The other end remained quiet.

Holly wondered if she was reflecting on her comments then offered in response.

"It seems you, and I have many secrets, Emily. And in light of this new hope you have brought me, I have a special secret for you to keep."

No, she hadn't thought it through, but Holly desperately wanted to share this news with another woman. No, the truth was, she wanted to share it with Kaine's sister.

Emily's curiosity peaked, and her voice carried the sound of a trustworthy friend.

"Don't tell me it has something to do with Luka?"

"On the contrary, it concerns your brother. As I said, a special secret."

"Don't worry if you mean, don't tell Kaine. He's too incommunicado these days."

Holly stole a long breath almost afraid to say the words aloud, fearing they may not come true. She summoned her courage and blurted out.

"I'm pregnant too!"

"No. How lovely," Emily flatly replied. The once friendly tone lost in disbelief, then leveled to a stoic reserve.

A British attitude Holly guessed. Holly pretended not to notice.

"Yes, I'm excited. I found out today. I thought the crummy way I've been dragging around a direct result of my injuries. But my doctor confirmed a few hours ago that I'm about seven weeks."

"I'm sorry to sound like I don't trust you. Am I to assume it's my brothers?" Emily's voice dropped to become so cold and smooth.

The defensive curls of being offended by Emily's referral to her unborn child as *it* set her thoughts to boil.

Holly won control over her shaking voice and made sure to keep her response light and even.

Chapter Fifteen

ABANDONED AND CONFUSED

How much worse were things going to get? Emily didn't wholeheartedly believe she carried her brother's baby.

What Holly explained, "If you're asking, have I've been with anyone else? NO! Emily, I haven't. I understand this situation doesn't look good for me. Especially, with my nude body plastered all over the world. But believe me, because of ghosts or demons of my own, whichever you would like to call them, they have prevented me from finding a tiny piece of happiness in Luka's warm, loving arms. And before Kaine, I hadn't been intimate with a man for years. In the end, the vivid memory of Kaine stepped in at the beach and stopped me."

Emily's tone softened, almost apologetic.

"I'm bloody sorry. I didn't mean to imply ... it's ... I know Kaine enforces a strict policy of using protection with all the diseases and loose tarts looking to file paternity suits. The last thing a man in Kaine's position needs is a paternity case brought against him from a one-off."

Holly wanted to drop her head into her hands and cry. Her

heart, indeed crushed, smashed to a pulp by Emily's indicting words. Her wonderful news twisted into something ugly. Their love affair, reduced to a one-off, indeed. She carried Kaine Walker's child. Conceived by Kaine, who begged her to have babies with him, start a family. Who wanted this child so badly the conception arrived with an uncontrollable passion the likes she'd never experienced.

Holly disappointment and rejection became difficult to banish from her tone of voice. Her spirits low, her damn disappointment at Emily's negative reaction running high. Holly changed the phone receiver to the other ear and drew in a sharp breath.

"Yes, Kaine is in a vulnerable position. I do understand. But for the record, I'm carrying Kaine's baby. I'll submit to any test you require. And remember, Kaine begged me to start a family. It would look like in the end he got what he wanted with me. Kaine made the choice when he took me quickly, his choice, Emily."

This time, whether Emily liked it or not, she would listen to the details of her brother's rash actions. After she'd unfolded her story of the unembellished behavior of her brother after the sound check in London, Emily backed away.

"That's unlike Kaine. I wonder?"

Holly noticed her voice softened and arrested Holly's curiosity.

"Wonder what?"

"It's clear, more than ever, that Kaine's deeply in love with you. I do know of his dreams of a family of his own. He does things unconventionally. It would be like him to capture you and take you away to start the family he wanted that badly. Can you forgive me, and my moment's doubt?"

Holly hesitated, confused by Emily's sudden change of heart. Emily understood this precious gift of a new life.

"Of course, it's hard for me to accept, but especially difficult for Luka." Damn! She shouldn't have said his name and couldn't stop the word from tumbling out.

"Luka?" Emily challenged. "What has that sod to do with your child?"

"Nothing, I assure you. He drove me to the doctor. He was there when I found out, for support, truly Emily."

Holly didn't dare mention Luka's rage when he discovered she would stand by Kaine. Or, the unmentionable fact that he offered to cover up her pregnancy and claim the child as his own.

Although, it didn't seem Luka would have shed a tear if she terminated the pregnancy. No, this was not the time to confess anymore to Emily. First, Holly wanted to make sure Emily believed she hadn't tried to arrange this pregnancy. And second, that she wasn't out to trap her world famous and sickeningly wealthy brother.

"What is important is that you believe my pregnancy is not of my doing. I told Kaine I didn't want to become pregnant by him, especially at the start of an eighteen-month world tour. I told him over and over again. No. No. That wasn't the best time to bring a child into the world. But it's happened, and my child is an incredible gift.

"What I need are answers.

"The hard questions you wonder.

"What do I do when the father of my baby and the man I love isn't here with me? Sometimes, I dream of getting on a plane and going to him. But even if I overcame the shame from London, I have the incriminating pictures at Malibu. How can I ever face him again?"

"Please, Holly! Forgive me. You're in a bloody awful situation. I've been stupid too. What you need is support, not criticism, and reprisal. Of course, you did not trick my brother and in my heart, I'm sure your love for Kaine is genuine. After London, you're standing up for your feelings for him. Any other woman would have a lawyer drawing up demands. I am happy. Let me take this incredible news to Kaine. He needs to know."

"No! Absolutely not! He comes back to me on his own, or I don't want him back at all!"

"Holly that's exceedingly noble, but a bit naïve. He's thousands of miles away. He's trapped on a worldwide tour and saddled with an active alcohol dependency and spiraling out of control into depression. How could he find the strength to fight that? How does he forget his demons from Briarwood? How does he happily skip down the path and straight back into your arms without something to strengthen him for the fight?"

Holly didn't have any answers. And she was sorry for her outburst to Emily.

"Holly, please, give Kaine something tangible to fight his way back."

"He has what he wants from me, my love, and a child. All we need Emily is a miracle."

"Yes indeed, a few miracles. The first one would be for Kaine to know he has your love because he doesn't. I can take that news to him. Then his love for you will be strengthened. I assume by the way you're talking you're keen on keeping his baby?"

"Yes! Never doubt that. And please don't take him the news that I love him. For the rest, I haven't any answers to the thousands of other questions you must have. I can't make any decisions until I can get distance and think for a while."

"I'm glad you're sensible. Please don't do anything rash without talking with me. We are a family Holly. You are carrying my niece or nephew. And as silly as this will sound to an American, if your child is male, he will be the first heir of your generation to inherit a royal title. And along with that, a great deal of land — Briarwood Estate. And don't forget all the other holdings of Kaine's. Either sex child will inherit close to half a billion dollars one day because of the *Hurrikaine* Corporation Kaine started with Nicky called LandFall Incorporated."

Holly didn't have a suitable response. She'd known Kaine would be worth a great deal of money, but half-billion dollars. A stunning amount! And her child would inherit what Luka called an empire.

As she regained her balance, she retorted.

"You're right Emily. At this moment, Kaine's royal title and financial assets mean nothing to me. They have no bearing on my decision. Remember, Kaine is an American, and it would appear he cares even less about his title as the Duke of Dunnehill."

"Listen carefully Holly. I understand this situation is uncomfortable and unsettling time. But Kaine may react differently about giving his son a choice to decline the title. This is your child's birthright. Beyond those points, your baby is of my bloodline. Our babies share a bloodline. They are cousins. Holly, you have to accept this. They are cousins, my child, and yours. This family already loves your child. Please, please let me tell Kaine.

"Your child is the tonic.

"Your child is your miracle.

"News of your child will bring him back to all of us."

Chapter Sixteen

COME UNDONE

Something inside Holly told her to resist the biting temptation to allow Emily to tell Kaine and live happily ever after. That warning dictated for her to state emphatically and to coupled it with a harsh tone.

"No. This news needed to be relayed to Kaine, in person, gently and lovingly by me. And he needs to come to me on his own. Otherwise, it would be worse if I never know why he came back."

Emily started to speak.

"No!" She repeated. "I mean it Emily! Kaine comes to me on his own, or NEVER!"

Half an hour later, Holly leaned back on a pile of pillows, her tears flowing freely. Her emotions resembled a train wreck. She lay watching Kaine kissing her passionately at the Hard Rock Café in London, for the hundredth time. Her thoughts strayed like confetti, picturing him alone in Europe, hurt and disillusioned with her. Yet she kept replaying her conversation with Emily.

One phrase stood out.

Kaine will be a smashing father.

No doubt. Holly remembered Kaine pampering and showering her with his love and gifts. She pictured him outside the castle playing with Tristan, Chris, the bass guitar player's son. How he'd laugh with ease and the joy that spread on his face, playing with Tristan. She wondered if telling Emily about her pregnancy had been in her best interest. Perhaps she wanted Emily to slip and tell Kaine the news and lift the impossible, heavy burden from her own tired shoulders. As usual, too many questions and not enough answers.

Holly lay on her bed wrapped in Kaine's jacket watching the music video. There would come a point, she would need to decide where she would have this baby if Kaine didn't come back for her. Would she stay in L.A., or go home to Santa Barbara and live with her parents until she carved out a new existence?

Blurting out this unexpected news to Emily canceled any future of Luka stepping in as a father to Kaine's heir. Unless, she married to Luka before Kaine found out. Which was impossible since Luka was already married! What a big complicated and muddled mess.

It occurred to her that Kaine might send his lawyers after her demanding custody of his child. She wouldn't stand a chance in Hell of winning up against Kaine's power and wealth. Her only chance then would be Luka, a certain financial match against Kaine.

Safeguarding her future was not looking good for her, to rely on Luka to take down Kaine. Her mind whirled on in mass confusion.

Of course, Kaine would insist he take part in his child's life. What about her? She'd never handle seeing Kaine if she married Luka, or worse if Kaine married?

Too many questions, no answers. But one thing was for sure. If Kaine came back to her, it couldn't be because she was pregnant.

Holly rewound the video to look at Kaine. What was not to love about her gorgeous man? And she made no mistake. The fog cleared. Her love grew stronger, and the baby changed nothing in her heart. Kaine was her man. Hadn't he told her she was the keeper of his heart? Perhaps Emily was correct. Kaine needed to go away from her — for a time. Get the tour out of his way. Release his demons. Or, he was merely playing out the hand she'd dealt him and doing what he needed ... and get over her.

"DAMN YOU!" She shouted at the screen suddenly remembering what happened in the corridor at Friar Manor. She continued to have flashes of Kaine and then he would fade like a puff of smoke. Luckily, the phone rang then to jar her from the memories. The Parisian accent was instantly calming.

"Holly, I was..." Solange's voice blared out of the answering machine.

Holly cut her off by picking up the receiver. She wondered if Emily called Solange. She wasn't going to change her mind.

Holly played the game, following Solange's lead.

They caught up on all the latest, except for her newest secret, hoping Emily kept her word. She'd already jeopardized her future by blurting it out to Emily.

Solange didn't waste much time.

"You've heard? Kaine, barely able to perform the night they played Copenhagen. He succeeded because he's a true professional. But Ian's worried. He's wondering how long Kaine will last. Kaine understands better than anyone the millions of dollars and hundreds of jobs resting on his usually competent shoulders.

"Nicky took over the day-to-day scheduling, and he's exhausted too. Ian is so concerned about the future of the *Hurrikaine* machine.

"I'm sure you won't be surprised to hear this. The reason I'm calling is Ian wanted me to ask about the vulgar photos. He can't understand and doesn't know how to fight them. Your nude body is all over Europe wrapped about Luka's."

Was there no end to the humiliation? But it was the way, Solange said, *wrapped around Luka's* that pushed Holly deeper into her shame. Her head bent as she winced from the lashes of guilt flogging her back.

"Solange, I'm sorry all these misperceptions happened. But there's nothing I can do about any of it."

As if she never heard Holly's explanation, Solange continued.

"According to Ian, the photos have sent Kaine off on another inspired depression. Apparently, people everywhere come up to taunt him about the Heart of the *Hurrikaine* on her knees before Luka. And for him to see you naked, making love with Luka. The press is worse in Europe. They've been unrelenting. It's hard for Kaine to fend off the insults about you. No one understands Holly, what the hell is going on between you and that duplicitous, lying, filthy bastard Luka?"

Holly didn't understand why everyone was quick to judge

Luka. What did he do to alienate him from everyone? Was leaving *Hurrikaine* such a tragedy? They should be glad he's gone since they feel antagonistic toward him. He'd given them more than a dozen years and taken the band to the top of their profession. Holly went over every detail with Solange, about the hot, sunny day in Malibu, which turned into her worst nightmare, wishing she'd never agreed to go to the beach to relax.

Predictably, Solange responded with the same prejudice as Emily. Holly wondered when she'd become such a poor judge of character? Her gut reactions always served her before, but that was before Luka Hunter, supposedly the master of emotions, the master at disguising his feelings.

"Holly you see Luka the way he wants. I've never known Luka to do anything without serving his purpose. Be very, very careful with Luka."

Holly turned a deaf ear. None of them spoke of experiencing Luka the way he treated her — loving and caring. He'd persisted, staying next to her during each step of the perilous journey into Hell. He was nothing short of an angel sent to guide her beyond the hellish darkness of rock music. But Solange repeated the same mantra as everyone associated with *Hurrikaine* believed.

"I'm surprised Luka didn't ignore your remark and make love with you to spite Kaine." Solange paused and then spoke in a softer, kinder voice.

"Maybe, he's changed, Holly. I doubt it, but whatever made him stop, I'm thankful. I shuddered to think what could have happened if you'd slept with Luka. Especially, with those photos splashed all over the world. The photos, you realize that because of them you'll never be free of Luka. And for all we know, you may have already lost Kaine for good."

"Thanks for the encouraging words Solange. Are you saying I have no future with Kaine?"

"I can't answer that."

The same old wall of condemnation surrounded her. The same urge to explain again. She started to plead with Solange as earlier with Emily. But she stopped. Enough was enough. She would only ask one favor.

"Please, I'm asking you to keep this to yourself. Please don't pass it on to Ian. Emily wanted to explain to Kaine, and I told her the same as you. Promise you won't tell Ian. I know what I'm doing. I have a few things to work out before Kaine hears the truth. And please, I'm not saying you are wrong, but there's innocence I share with Luka. Please, try to understand, it wasn't Luka's fault. If it's anyone's, it's mine."

"Are you crazy? If you wait, Kaine may not care what you have to say. Do you honestly know what you are asking me to promise by keeping quiet? From Kaine's point of view, you're sleeping with his enemy. You do understand Holly. Kaine is in love with you. More than you seem to realize. Why else would he care what the hell you do? Wake up, Holly! Before it's too late to repair."

"I'll stay optimistic in your assessment of Kaine's feelings for me. And, after all, this latest bad press, I do hope he loves me. You don't know how much I needed to hear that."

"Well, all is not lost. Emily and I hold out that you will have come to your senses when you see Kaine. By then you'll be able to talk things out with him in person."

"See Kaine?" She repeated.

Her heart started to beat loudly against her chest, threatening to break free. She would see Kaine soon.

"Where? When?" Holly tried to keep the rush of adrenaline in check.

"At my wedding on December 31st, in Pasadena at the New Rochelle Hotel, of course. Kaine is Ian's best friend, remember, like brothers. Holly, please tell me you did realize Kaine would be the best man. Remember, you've already given your pledge to be my bridesmaid. You'll have to see him then if only for a few moments to take pictures with him as members of the wedding party. I'm sure Ian and I can arrange a private meeting somewhere for the two of you."

Holly couldn't stop the joy that filled her heart. She wanted to do handsprings and skip up a flowered lane. She would see her Precious One. Yes!!!

Holly calmed her voice. "You're right, of course. But Solange, it has never crossed my mind that I would see him again, considering he lives in England."

Holly heard little after Solange's bombshell. Eventually, she agreed to show up for the first of many bridesmaid gown fittings. They hung up, and Holly quickly calculated she would be almost four months pregnant when she saw Kaine. She shouldn't be showing enough to influence any feelings he may hold for her.

This was a staggering but fantastic new development. She had an exact day, place, and time where she would next see her ex-lover-fiancé. Kaine. She would have to work beyond her feelings of shame and betrayal by then. She wondered what he would think when he learned he would see her again. Would his love disintegrate into hate, after all, the negative publicity with Luka? Would he avoid her? Or, would he forgive her and be willing to work things out with her?

Holly's mind raced with romantic scenarios of the two of them lost in each other rekindling their forever love. She'd bring him home to her bed, high in the canyon, as she dreamed of too many times before everything went wrong.

Then she remembered Luka. How happy would he be knowing Kaine would be at the wedding?

Damn!

He already knew.

She'd bet money on it.

He'd been anticipating the reunion ... Luka, always far ahead of her — but then, so did Kaine.

They both knew.

The confrontation date — December 31st.

As usual, everyone knew but her.

That's what Emily meant.

I could only hope once he overcomes this dark melancholy he will summon his courage and go to L.A., for you. And Luka is counting on this. It will be the last confrontation. Honestly, I fear the outcome, whoever leaves this final round without you will surely perish.

Holly had scoffed believing Emily's reaction as overly dramatic! But Emily saw the potential for disaster.

How was Holly going to get through the next eight long weeks?

Kaine was coming....

Chapter Seventeen

WITH OR WITHOUT

Holly awoke, soaked in a pool of sweat. Her phone rang out loudly. The answering machine clicked on, and she listened.

"Hello, Holly? Solange. Damn! Please, don't have left. Please, pick up the phone."

"Solange, what is it? What's happened?"

"I just hung up from Ian. I have news."

"Good. I hope Kaine is doing better?"

"Somewhat, yes. Ian returned from an impromptu studio session with Kaine. Kaine wrote a new song to record, and get this title, "Cold Without You." Ian's positive it's about you. He says it's Kaine's finest work yet. That means the last two songs the man wrote were for you."

Holly couldn't hear Solange.

She remembered one cold, early morning in Kaine's suite when the words flowed easily sitting by the window, pouring out her heart. She'd quickly scrawled the lyrics on a concert program while Kaine slept. Yes, "Cold Without You" was her song all right — her song, her lyrics, not Kaine's.

What's worse?

Kaine recorded the song. She heard Solange's excited voice. But everything was wrong.

"I'm positive the song is for you," Solange asserted to encourage Holly.

If she only knew the truth.

"Yes, yes, I suppose it's my song."

It's cold without you, my Precious One.

And Holly remembered they'd been the last words she'd spoken to Kaine backstage at Friar Manor before all hell broke loose. She drifted back to Solange saying.

"That makes *two* songs!" Solange repeated.

"Two?" Holly lost track of the conversation.

"Ian said they put the finishing touches on "My Lady." But because of Kaine's broken hand, Ian is playing acoustic guitar while Kaine plays the haunting melody on the piano with his strong hand. Ian said Kaine sang straight from his broken heart. That Kaine wants to release a mini-CD package of the two songs and donate the proceeds to help people convicted of crimes they haven't committed, of all things. Where does he get these ideas?

"Then Kaine surprised Ian with the staggering news that he was giving this recording his best effort because he didn't know how long he could keep going. Luckily, CMT videotaped the session for a music video. Otherwise, they would be without footage of Kaine.

"Ian said Kaine's not eating. The depression is winning. He doesn't know how much longer this tour is going to continue and eager to finish the few dates left in Eastern Europe. Kaine's put a halt to adding on dates, as they customarily plan.

"And Holly, Ian tried to explain to Kaine about you and Luka. I'm sorry, I had to tell Ian, and he wouldn't take no for an answer. Ian's been the target of the press too, he understands. He wanted to explain because Kaine sits and plays your song," Solange apologetically explained.

Holly sat crying in silence, pulling on her stud earring. She only sat and played their video — what a pair they were. And she knew why he picked the defense fund. She'd told him that they could build a new future, helping others that beautiful day long ago at Briarwood. But one thing for sure, Kaine was reaching out, sending her a message — if she could decipher it.

"Holly? Holly? Are you all right?"

"Yes." A tiny gust of air pushed the whispered word out. She cleared her throat confessing yet again.

"I've sure made a mess of things."

"It takes two Holly or maybe three, in this case. You didn't do this alone. Don't you see? Kaine has to love you to be in this much pain and conflict. Holly please, you need to reconsider."

"Reconsider what? There's nothing else I can do."

Defeat laced Solange's voice as she changed the subject to when she was coming down to L.A. And before she hung up, Solange showered Holly with the obligatory warnings.

"Be cautious and very, very careful of Luka."

Holly said goodbye, feeling torn up and confused.

An hour later, Holly arrived at CMT, and the atmospheres was electric. She wore a moss-green tailored jacket with black braided trim and an onyx colored mini skirt with the black

Prada pumps. She'd left her hair hanging long and straight, held back with a black velvet clip.

Luka met her at the elevator. Only this time, his usual sunny smile seemed unable to cheer her up her dark mood. His sparkling blue eyes accented, light blue, stonewashed jeans and a midnight-blue denim shirt with black leather elbow patches, and his Gucci loafers. He stole her breath away. All while his sensual body screamed touch me, love me, and trust me. But she'd experienced a rough morning. Making love wasn't going to happen today.

Luka whisked her away to an emergency meeting with Michael. The awful cloud of heavy despair lifted. Holly tried to sound cheerful. The first thing she noticed — Michael's cologne lingering like a light mist, flooding her with the usual painful memories. The second thing she noticed was how comfortable and approachable he was considering his commanding position at CMT.

During the last year, CMT made or destroyed any band they wanted by adding rotations of a single or freezing them out. And though COO was printed on his letterhead, she was suspicious of his title. Luka seemed more authoritative, according to the way Michael would look to Luka for approval. However, Michael could do as he pleased with her and she wondered what he wanted this time.

Michael didn't waste any time letting her know.

"Please, sit down, Holly. We want you to look at the dailies of "My Lady," Kaine's next release."

Holly sat, stunned by his words sinking sluggishly into the soft, leather chair. Luka walked over and hit the play button. The torturous viewing of the video on the widescreen

TV started a countdown in her mind, strapped in, about to blast off into the empty space of Kaine. There was no escaping this new barrage of tortures. She closed her eyes briefly to gather her composure. She opened her eyes.

Damn!

Kaine, in another black and white film noir, singing "My Lady," the song he wrote declaring his love for her.

Kaine sat lost and alone in the dark, empty recording studio. A single candle burned in front of him, sitting on the edge of the piano. Her heart skipped a beat, her last breath already forgotten, as she listened to his genius.

His face was half lit by the white candlelight, making him incomparably handsome. Yes, he was, even more, beautiful, so devastatingly handsome wearing a banded collared shirt, light in color, unbuttoned as far as she could see. But it did not open for her to catch a glimpse of his scrumptious chest. His black hair hung long, below his shoulders and his sideburns trimmed, revealing his earlobe, where he continued to wear the diamond stud. She instinctively pulled on her ear.

His chin sported a closely cropped beard, yet his eyes were filled with anguish. And when he looked into the camera, his eyes told the entire story of a lonely man, cast adrift alone to face his private terrors. She wished she could reach out and hold him, love him and comfort him, like every woman in the world would want to do.

She sucked in a breath and put on her best mask to hide the gamut of emotions as they flooded her mind and then surely her face. She must not let Luka or Michael see them.

"Women all over the world are going to eat this up around the clock. Women love to save a man from himself. And

Kaine has the public sympathy after the photos at the beach. He's going to make us all a lot of money off of this tragedy. But here is the reason I wanted you to see this," Michael said matter-of-factly, as he glanced nervously to Luka, who gave the signal to go ahead.

"I understand "My Lady" was written for you. The publicity department collected all the publicity clips of you and Kaine in London and more on Kaine in Europe. I have the recent headlines screaming for more about Kaine and his Mystery Lady — you."

Michael pointed out pragmatically as he glanced again over to Luka.

"The London response to you and Kaine in the "Now that I've Found You" video was phenomenal and shot to number one in the requests during the first hour. Clive…"

Holly politely interrupted, "Clive?"

"Sorry, Clive Sherwood is CEO in London at the CMT-UK affiliate. He reports the response was overwhelming for CMT-UK. Clive is delighted you have become the Cinderella story come true. The Mystery Lady Hooks Royal Rocker! Not since the commoner married the Prince of England, has this kind of heavy press been generated.

"The scandalous news has created an unprecedented *Hurrikaine* record purchasing frenzy, and the last concerts are sold out. The public demands details about you. They are press starved. You Miss Hill are in demand. Luka wants to promote quickly because you are a tremendously hot item."

Michael glanced up to Luka as if to seek his approval. Then he looked at Holly as if he expected her to comment.

A hot item, she thought.

Was that what she was to Luka? Finally, the agenda everyone suspected? It couldn't be — she hoped. She looked to Luka with guarded eyes. Luka's face was a mask, revealing nothing.

Michael continued in the background.

"This is why I, I mean *we,* want you to consider this proposal. We would like your permission to edit parts of the footage from London, into the "My Lady" video. Luka and I have been in meetings all morning with the executives of *Hurrikaine's* personal label, LandFall Management Company, Incorporated (LMC). Nicky Jamison stepped in as COO of LMC and agreed to support whatever Luka's decided and turned the entire project over to him."

Why wasn't she surprised?

Luka stood and raised his eyebrows and sheepishly looked down at Holly.

"Since CMT owns most of the original footage shot with you in it, we will use certain portions of the video, and I hope this doesn't embarrass you. We want to use the close up where you are, well, gazing into each other's eyes. We have it ready."

It was everything she could do to remember to breathe.

Why was Luka doing this to her?

Was this some sort of test?

Would she pass?

What would Luka do to her if she didn't pass?

There was Kaine again. She could see how much in love with her he'd been. No one needed to convince her, it was there for the entire world to see.

Kaine Walker loved her. It was there in his eyes, the film didn't lie. It captured the honesty of his love.

Holly fell into their dream, lost in the magic of the moment, barely noticing, far in the background Michael speaking

"We want to edit in film clips of Kaine in concert with shots juxtaposition to you. We'll have a spectacular video! I am waiting for the dailies from Europe. I'm told CMT-UK videotaped both sessions of "My Lady" and a second song, I understand we'll love."

"Yes, "Cold Without You." Holly volunteered as if a zombie. She never noticed Michael's confused reaction to her exclusive news.

Luka did.

"Yes, that's the title I have here." Michael checked the fax on his desk. Then Michael looked to Luka with a puzzled look.

Even Luka flashed a look of wonderment on his usually composed face.

She watched his eyes slide to the side. They said *WHO* was she in touch with to have the confidential information?

Holly lifted her glance from Luka to Michael.

"I'm in touch."

"That's good," Michael stuttered. "Holly, are you on board with being a part of the new video?" He'd said more to confirm than asked.

It didn't make any difference. She wasn't going to fool anyone. Of course, it was all right. She and Kaine belonged together, and nobody could stop them.

Luka sent her a supportive wink.

The possibilities astounded her.

She and Kaine to be reunited on celluloid — once again.

Chapter Eighteen

PICTURES OF YOU

Holly cranked up her car speaker volume to ten to blast "Now That I've Found You." The haunting song blared from passing cars, at the office, and seemingly every ten minutes on CMT. Everywhere Holly went that song played. The ballad rocked the charts. CMT placed the video in the enviable rotation position of running once every hour. "Now That I've Found You" was a raging rocket into the music stratosphere.

There was nowhere to run, nowhere to hide from Kaine. Everyone she encountered wore that same hard, accusatory look. Stranger's eyes said, *"I know you're fucking Luka."*

The girls snickered behind her back at CMT, and people on the street that recognized her yelled, "Hey mystery lady, let's have a look!"

Her parents understood, as usual, and tried to encourage her by saying she'd be old news by the weekend. It was the single most humiliating stretch of time in her life. She went to sleep that night thinking how luck would have it. She was to turn twenty-nine the next day, the day of the edit on "My

Lady." Kaine would be twelve thousand miles away.

Nevertheless, she would be twenty-nine and appear by the magic of editing, in her second music video! Who would have believed last summer, working behind the scenes with Brett on the Collins murder trial that she would become the focus of international attention and in a mega-hit music video?

Holly awoke drowsy on her birthday. She always needed more sleep, but Luka expected her to be at CMT to assist him and oversee the editing. It was Saturday, and unusually hot. She dressed casually in a dark mauve chamois and camel colored walking shorts. She added Espresso-colored leather sandals and a new black *Hurrikaine* baseball cap that reminded her of her situation stitched across the front — *Illusions of Self,* the new album title. She arrived at CMT without makeup and her hair damp, tossed up in a ponytail.

It wasn't long before Luka slid up behind her. His fresh scent washed over her like a sweet, summer breeze. First came the warm moisture of his breath. Then his lips barely touched the lobe of her ear, sending incredible waves of tingling sensations up and down ordering bumps to rise up on her skin.

"Miss Hill, you look beautiful. You remind me of how much of a man I am and what a wonderful woman you are," he gently complimented.

He moved around in front of her, his body brushing hers. Her nipples harden thinking about how wonderful he was too. He tossed her a sparkling wink, and a small twinge of guilt assaulted, reminding her how tremendously attracted to him. Unfortunately, the chemistry was more powerful than ever. And she couldn't understand why? Was it because he had become forbidden? Was it simply that Emily and Solange were jealous of her attention from Luka? His recent change in behavior seemed to put everyone on edge. Had he simply fallen in love with her and he'd become a reformed man? Stranger things happened.

Perhaps Luka never praised and cared for them as he did her? He was damn near impossible to resist, and difficult to shift her glance off him, taking the exquisite picture of him to be locked away forever in her mind? She smiled quickly, accepting his continued appraisal of her with his eyes sweeping her body. When they leveled and stared straight into hers, she saw the passion, the desire, and lust to take her right then and there. But she'd learned the hard way. Luka was a gentleman with her, worse, yet an English gentleman. And he did not entertain public displays of his affections with her.

Luka surrendered to the hot, Santa Ana winds. His clothing choice delighted her, wearing a black, silk vest, with nothing beneath it, but his sun-kissed, tanned, muscular chest. Her eyes followed his shapely arms as they crossed over his chest as she admired the valley of his muscles. His sparse blond chest hair peeked over the edge of his vest, inviting her to run her fingertips over him. His slim legs clad in fitted black Levi's. He was sockless in black deck shoes.

He instantly melted her vow of restraint. California casual looked absolutely delicious on Luka. He was soooooo tempting. He looked good enough to eat with his freshly washed, long blonde hair, sparkling in contrast to the black, John Roberts, baseball cap pushed back on his head.

She didn't want to suffer the torture and complete madness that made less sense each time she was around him.

Predictably, her mind switched channels. Time to direct

her thoughts to her future. She looked up at him and found gentleness and softness in his incredible blue eyes. She stored the always attractive picture of Luka back in her mind. But her heart reminded it belonged to Kaine. She closed her eyes to kiss Luka quickly, barely touching his lips.

No, she hadn't abandoned Luka.

Chapter Nineteen

RUNNING ON FAITH

Holly leaned against the wall of the editing room. It had been a long day. She massaged her aching foot when an intern brought her a long, gold box. Luka trailed the young man and moved closer, his facial expression was indifferent, his eyes curious. He was doing an unbelievably poor job of covering his interest. Were they from *him*? And he wanted to watch her reaction?

Luka had never given her flowers. Not like Kaine. Kaine loved to shower her with flowers. He'd filled entire suites in London with roses, twice. She released a small sigh, remembering rose petals sprinkled all over the bed in the castle bedchamber where they'd make love and vowed never to leave each other. Back when they were so naïve as to have faith in a pledge and a promise to fight Luka together and that the pledge would win.

But it hadn't. Here she was with Luka.

How quickly the beautiful memories disintegrate into the ugliness of the past and the truth hurt like hell. Their love hadn't been strong enough to survive Luka. She looked over to him. Her heart tightened as it flip-flopped. Where would she be without him?

Pregnant and alone!

She smiled, realizing his immediate curiosity wasn't to see the pleasure on her face, but because he didn't know who'd sent them. He wanted to know who was that intimate that they would send this large box of flowers. She decided to let him wonder a moment. She pulled the tiny card from its holder. She released a warm sigh. They were from her parents and the card brought a flush of happy tears.

For our angel.
One, for each year of joy you have brought us.
Love, Mom, and Dad.

"Excuse me? Good news?" Luka inquired quickly, brushing his body against hers, putting her on alert. She was amused by his insecurity. It was good to see a bit of his propriety shaken loose from his calm veneer, like a curling paint chip on a piece of priceless wood.

Holly smiled, and then softly laughed.

"Had you going? These are from my parents." She laughed again and leaned into him.

He good-naturedly allowed her this familiarity, letting her know she'd caught him off guard.

The intimate act endeared him to her that he would allow her to see a vulnerable moment. It was true. She may be his only weakness.

He caught himself and smiled his sunny Luka smile.

"Congratulations on your new post at CMT, or the baby?"

He asked casually. His innocent comment robbing her of the momentary high.

"No, not the baby, I haven't told my parent's anything. After I'd found the courage to call and explain Malibu, I couldn't confess I was pregnant too, especially by a man they've never met. They would be sure to assume my baby was yours. You know Dad. He's great, a real liberal until it comes to his daughter he becomes protective with issues concerning me and to have me pregnant, with the father ten thousand miles away, wouldn't set well with him."

Luka moved his head in agreement. She saw the flash of surprise cross Luka's face when she'd said the *baby was yours*. She could tell he'd think she'd made a decision to let him father her child. Later she would explain that she would tell her dad Kaine was the father. Telling Emily sealed that fate. Though, bearing Luka's baby wouldn't be a terrible fate either, perhaps after this child. What a ludicrous idea — to give birth to both Luka's and Kaine's children!

She shuddered at the preposterous idea.

But her father expressed a strong fondness for Luka. To produce a room full of children with Luka would bring complete happiness to her parents. Yes, her mother adored Luka with his charms, good manners, but mostly she'd said, for the devotion she saw in Luka's eyes for her only daughter.

"Would it have been too bloody hard to tell them you're carrying my child?"

Holly hadn't anticipated Luka would attempt to change her mind about naming Kaine as father. Thrown off guard, she managed to say.

"I can't answer that question."

And what she didn't say was that could never be. That would be another time because Emily knew the truth. She wanted to add that there was nothing wrong with him fathering a child with her, but would have to be his. Not Kaine's as his. When the time came, her parents would be delighted to learn Luka was going to become their new son-in-law. And then excited that she was planning to raise a family with him.

But Luka needed to ask her first.

And before that, he had to be divorced!

And before that, Kaine couldn't come back for her.

Luka took the hint she wasn't changing her mind and changed the subject.

"Birthday then? When is your birthday? Surely, not today?" His facial expression spread taut as if confused and caught off guard again. Twice in the space of fifteen minutes, didn't set well as he clenched his jaw. Luka Hunter prided himself on his attention to detail.

"Yes, a wonderful birthday, spending it with you."

Luka stepped closer, breaking his resolution to stay apart. His arms snaked around her waist, and he pulled her quickly behind a tall, large trunk with cables spilling out of it. His lips came within a breath of hers. Their breath mixed creating a new scent.

Her body poured like liquid gold into a mold, filling the curves of his body, the heat between them growing.

"I beg to differ with you Miss Hill. This is a long way from what you deserve. Today is a celebration. Please, say you'll allow me to show you an enchanting evening?"

Then he backed away.

"How presumptuous of me, naturally, you have other plans."

The burning heat scorched her cheeks.

"I'm embarrassed to report, I was planning to go home and soak in a hot, bubbly bath, after bending over editing machines."

She tried to drop her chin.

But Luka caught it in his hand. He tilted her chin up to him until her gaze leveled on him.

And she couldn't understand if what he was doing was sincere. To have his attention and affection had been far from her wants and needs that morning, she'd climbed on the plane to run away to London, never realizing she would meet *him.* Or, dare to believe he would come to care for her.

And he did.

The astonishing changes in her life happened because she'd chosen to take a chance with Luka because he'd been too beautiful, too perfect to let get away. And oh, those blue eyes of his could never lie to her about that. He may not say the words, but every day he was around her, she knew he was learning to live with her. Learning what made her happy, brought her joy, or brought her pain. Soon he would never want to live without her.

"I won't bloody well have that, at a minimum, dinner, and dancing."

Oh, the promise in those words, bringing possibilities later of a long night of exquisite, passionate love. Butterflies suddenly tickling her stomach because she would never say no to his invitation. But to stand and dance?

"I don't know if I have anything formal to wear for dinner

and dancing."

Luka leaned close to her ear. "I'll have something sent here. Trust me, you'll be dressed perfectly."

"But Luka." She tried to protest.

"I'll be back straightaway," he promised and then sprinted out the door.

She walked down to the commissary to grab a decaffeinated coffee, wondering where to draw on the requisite energy needed to keep up with Luka. She looked over and saw a group of women obviously gossiping about her. Ironically, she carried a decadent reputation for something she would never have predicted, for sleeping with beautiful men, and one right after the other, two men closer than brothers.

She recalled Kaine's plea in the castle, telling her that terrible stories being reported and written about him that weren't true. And to always ask him for the truth. And here it happened to her, lies all about her. No one bothered to ask her if it the stories were true. Or had she bedded both? If only that were true.

The papers didn't have the facts, and the scandal had blown up out of proportion quickly. She'd joined the ranks of the outlaws, and that meant big money offered for any picture of her to plaster on a tabloid cover. A few papers condemned her others commended her on the affair with Luka.

Her love affairs seemed to stir up controversy and speculation. Everyone offered an opinion about her and Luka's love happened and what their future should be. How did anyone know? She'd been there, and she didn't. But it happened, and every facet of her life was up for grabs to the highest bidder. And nothing she could do would change that. She smiled, remembering how one tabloid claimed her to be Luka's newest lover. Perhaps after tonight, she would live up to her Lolita reputation.

She gripped her knee, digging her nails in to stop the thoughts. She was glad the task-at-hand ended. She sat, very, very tired, and her hand magnetically went to cover her stomach.

"Yes, little one, you soak up all my energy. How like your father you already are."

She smiled and whispered, "My baby, Kaine's baby." She dropped the coffee cup in the nearest trash container and then returned to the editing room to find a woman waiting from the wardrobe department.

"Luka asked me to give you these and instructed me to tell you to dress and wait for him. There are a hair stylist and make-up artist due any minute. Hurry, it wouldn't do to keep Luka waiting."

No, it would never do, Holly thought.

She opened the large golden box with the black Asset logo splattered across the top. Inside, she discovered a black velvet dress. No — gown was a better choice of words. She quickly stripped out of her clothes and into the glove-tight gown. She looked over into a small broken mirror to discover a strapless, heart-shaped bodice, struggling to hold in her full breasts. A slit cut high on the side of her thigh showed more leg than she was used to revealing. She sucked in a breath, trying to learn how to hold her lithe frame in the demanding dress. How could Luka believe she could pull off this charade as a lady of grace and fine breeding?

The hairstylist and make-up artist arrived, and when they'd left, her shiny, sable hair hung straight and sleek down her back almost touching her waist. Her face looked like she'd had a refreshing nap. She reached into the box to discover a pair of elbow length black, silk gloves. In the corner, she noticed a turquoise velvet box. Inside a diamond teardrop necklace from Tiffany's sat for her approval.

They must be on loan, she thought, they'd easily cost six figures.

Holly stepped into the black, silk spiked heels wondering why he'd selected these. Surely, her back would hurt after hours of dancing in these.

A loud ruckus behind her attracted her attention. Luka walked in dressed to impress, black as midnight. He looked stunning in a black, tailored Asset suit, a soft, black fitted shirt covering his chest, sockless with black Gucci suede loafers, casual and yet impossibly handsome.

Holly wasn't sure when Luka became her entire world. Or, exactly when the sparkle in his blue eyes came to mean everything to her?

The scent of him reached her. She thought of the past for one last second because Luka was coming for her. She couldn't imagine her life without him anymore. Even though she carried the precious gift of life inside her, she didn't have the same intense, daily bond, with Kaine, as she did with Luka. When was it, she'd fallen into this strange love and adoration for Luka? Which hour, which minute?

That didn't matter anymore, what did, this moment — when she realized Luka Hunter was the only man in her life. The only man to stand by her and give her the necessary strength and support to raise a child. He'd given her a job, given her freedom to love him, and not be haunted by the ghost of Jon de La Guerra, and then Kaine Walker. Her family adored him as she did.

Luka Hunter.

She willed her heart to try to open to him.

However, adoration was not true love.

Luka took one more step closer to stand inches away. His usually flowing hair was pulled back into a tail, exposing his tiny ears, and in his left lobe, hung a tiny gold hoop.

Luka was breathtaking.

He bent at his waist and in a tone of promise, "My beautiful Miss Hill, we have until midnight."

"What happens then?"

"I make you scream...."

Chapter Twenty

ALWAYS

Luka handed Holly a small black box with a silver bow. "For you. I've arranged special reservations for an exclusive dinner celebration for you. If we leave now, we'll have time to make it."

Holly hurriedly pulled the ribbon from the box. Under layers of tissue, she discovered a pair of flat, black velvet slippers.

"The first of many comforts." He smiled and winked at her as only he could.

She laid her hand against Luka's smooth cheek and then followed an impulse to confess. "I do need you, Luka Hunter."

"I hope you do Babe, I hope you do."

"You're always there for me, aren't you?" Holly confirmed, stroking his smooth freshly shaven face.

"Always," Luka agreed his blue eyes flashing as he stepped next to her. He'd wetted his lips with a flick of his tongue seconds before he pressed them against hers, brushing her lightly. His arms snaked around her body, as his passion grew, threatening to overcome him. His sudden display of emotion for the world to see spoke volumes. He quickly released her, straightened his spine, and slipped on his Ray Ban sunglasses. He threw her a sexy grin, took her hand, and led her out to his convertible Corvette and put down the top.

Luka slipped away with her in the silent twilight driving over the Santa Monica Mountains to the San Fernando Valley, down Hollywood Way, to the entrance of the Burbank Airport.

He grinned mischievously and suggested.

"I have the CMT jet awaiting my instructions."

"The jet?"

He didn't answer.

"Where are we headed?"

"Let me surprise you."

Holly agreeably sat back in the luxurious CMT jet, absolutely amazed at his resourcefulness, knowing he could take her anywhere in the world. He was a remarkable man.

The plane landed twenty minutes later at the Santa Barbara Airport.

"You're taking me home?"

"Close, I have a surprise of my own."

A new, forest-green, Range Rover, awaited Luka on the tarmac. The drive down the Pacific coast to the small Mediterranean styled town was lovely. The sun's intention clear, ready to slip into the clear, blue Pacific Ocean, exactly like the color of Luka's eyes.

Holly watched the exit signs pass. Many happy childhood memories popped into her mind. She loved Santa Barbara, and she wished she lived by the peaceful ocean. The water always gave her strength, and in those idle moments, she set about a new plan. She would raise her child near the cool, serene, water's edge. And knew she could count on Luka to help her make it happen. She smiled a satisfied grin, unable to remember the last time she'd experienced peace.

"This is perfect Luka. I needed to be home."

Luka pulled into a parking space in the quaint Santa Barbara marina parking lot. He pulled out a plastic parking card and insisted.

"You need to put all your cares away for one night and relax. Come, we have another chance to watch another sunset together. I promised you a thousand sunsets, and I am a man of my word."

Holly smiled, bent over, and quickly kissed his soft lips.

"How did I get so lucky?"

"I'm the lucky one Babe."

Luka stopped the car and faced her while unbuckling his seat belt. He leaned closer, and she saw his gentle blue eyes reminding her of his faithfulness and love. His breath sweet, inviting. Luka pressed his lips against hers, taking his time until they molded to hers perfectly, while the tip of his tongue gently dueled with hers, telling her to relax and that when she was ready, he would love her, and only then.

Luka pulled away too fast. His beautiful hooded eyes opened. His breath ragged and husky, overcome by his desire for her that left him breathless.

"When you kiss me, I forget who and what I am. I become a man I've long forgotten," he confessed with ease.

Holly was sure her face flushed with a bright scarlet color. And his kiss, his forceful kiss lingered on her lips.

Luka turned off the engine and stepped out of the car. He strolled with her hand-in-hand, along the beach walk, beyond the personal access gate and then along a row of boat slips.

"Is everything going well?" Luka asked smoothly out of the blue.

"If you're referring to my pregnancy, I have the typical symptoms. My body's exceptionally sensitive, tender. Nausea comes and goes. To be expected. That's why I'm glad we're not going to make a big night of it."

"Who say's we're not?" He looked down at her and winked.

A second flash of embarrassment arrived, wondering how far he intended to carry this night. She was too tired and would never have the strength to say no.

"Is this where the dinner celebration is? The Marina? I've always enjoyed a good wine and the seafood dinners served at the wharf."

"Close, a private and exclusive dinner aboard my boat, Miss Hill, is what you bloody well need."

She understood he was capturing her, taking her away from everything she knew to be alone with him.

Luka extended his hand to escort her up the steps. She looked up and down the rows of sailboats, catamarans, and yachts of all sizes.

What could Luka afford, she wondered.

He stopped in front of a small yellow speedboat.

She chuckled, picturing them sitting at the helm, dressed to kill in their diamonds and velvet.

Luka helped her, holding her hand.

Holly smiled, keeping her disappointment to herself.

Luka stepped up to the wheel and smoothly guided the boat out into the harbor.

Holly relaxed, letting her long hair, blow freely in the sea breeze, wondering where the mysterious Luka Hunter would take her. How far out to sea did he intend to take her to be alone? She couldn't help dreaming how tender and loving Luka was when the world couldn't see him. Until this moment, she hadn't realized how much the photos of Malibu must have disturbed him too, and the thought disgusted her. The searing shame hurt for being self-absorbed, ignoring his reactions to the slimy press. It was his body laid out for the world to see too. The world saw his face with her on her knees before him.

What a nightmare she'd brought to his life? Never once had he complained. She hadn't been aware enough to ask, and that admission slapped her hard motivating her to understand Luka's sacrifices by showing him respect. To tell him she appreciated him creating trust, well-being, and the comfortable life he'd designed though he'd known her eight short weeks.

They passed through a thick patch of fog. She didn't notice they'd descended upon a vessel until too late. Luka slowed to a stop alongside an enormous yacht. Her mouth dropped open, and she tasted the cool sea mist. It had to be well over a hundred feet long. This was the longest ship, she'd ever seen in the harbor. Yes, it certainly dwarfed the luxurious Templeton yacht. She held her hand out in awe as Luka escorted her up to the deck.

She tried to speak without sounding too impressed, she emphasized in a feathery whisper.

"This is your BOAT?"

Holly was barely able to swallow a nervous laugh.

"Yes, I suppose so," he impishly answered, flashing a sly smile.

"I see what you mean. That is a bit of an understatement."

He joined in easily laughing with her, sharing one of his joyous full-bodied laughs that lit up the universe.

"I saw it one day, said I wanted it. The next day Kaine had it delivered."

Kaine.

How the word hung on her heart instantly. She shook off the grievous feelings. What if Kaine Walker had millions to lavish on the people he loved? She looked at Luka. He was laughing. He hadn't realized what he'd said. The gift a sweet memory for him, and she wouldn't take that moment away from him for anything. She'd bet he would lie instead of admitting he missed Kaine too.

It was good to see him laughing, and she realized he seldom did. This trying time had been hard on him. How selfish she'd been wrapped up in herself.

Luka.

Always forced to anticipate her comfort first, but then, wasn't that what love was?

Luka gently laid his arm on her shoulder while she canvassed the gorgeous Santa Barbara landscape. The lights started to twinkle along the shoreline. A fitting backdrop with the mountains standing majestically, witnessing this special moment with Luka.

"Another sunset, my luv."

Holly leaned back against him. She'd heard his sweet words.

My luv.

And at that moment, she hated Kaine.

Holly was hollow, no love or comfort to give Luka all

these weeks. Kaine stole her empathy all like a thief in the night leaving her empty and useless. Kaine had blasted into her life, loving her in an unimaginable fashion, and she'd never forget him. And their affair made no sense, while Luka waited, biding his time. She hoped she could keep the ghost of Kaine behind her and not have Luka wait too much longer.

"Another beautiful sunset." She pointed out as their moment passed. Then she questioned as suddenly as the thought swept into her mind.

"Isn't this where Tessa said she was staying?"

"Yes, but she is in San Francisco for a few days. No doubt looking to hire the best solicitor to cut off my bleedin'...."

He stopped and swallowed.

He lowered his voice, "... to start the divorce proceedings. Exhibit one — those awful bloody photos. I dread it, yet, I'll be free, to start a bright, new future. I've been expecting a notice from her thieving solicitors. I wonder what misery she is conjuring up for me."

"You're concerned Tessa's demands will be unacceptable?" At once, Holly wanted to chastise herself, realizing she'd never listen to Luka's personal problems.

"No. I want to be armed the moment they arrive. I've hired a team of hard-hitting solicitors to assist the CMT legal staff, to sue the rag papers for what they have done to us."

He stepped back and took in a deep breath of sea air while leaning his elbow on the railing. His hair blew back off his face. He was half man, half God, rising up out of the ocean. And the sight of him left her with chills. The moonlight brushed his delicate features like highlights on a master's painting.

"Enough of me and the business," he stated dismissing his thoughts. "This is your special night."

Luka took her hand and led her on a tour of his boat named the Day Dreamer. It was everything she'd expected the oversized luxury liner to be, spacious and comfortable. There was a fully stocked bar, yet they sipped mineral water as they sat behind the wheel. Luka steered the ship deeper into the calm, open sea heading toward the Channel Islands. He stopped short of them, under the full, autumn moon, mammoth and inviting almost as if one could reach out and touch it.

The ship gently swayed, dancing with the calm sea, rocking her like a baby in a cradle. Yes, Holly relaxed, at peace, when the crew of two made their presence known. These men were on Luka's payroll, and they knew better than to allow anything to disturb his privacy. One crew member, Patrick, who undoubtedly doubled as a bodyguard, took over the helm while a second man named Pierce, dressed in a tuxedo, arrived to discuss the special dinner cuisine with Luka.

Pierce, graced with an English accent, somewhere in his forties, was well trained with impeccable manners. He set an elegant table in an enclosed glass area on the forward deck through though the night air was unseasonably warm for a fall evening. The harvest moon joined a galaxy of twinkling stars that lit the sky as the gentle sea breeze swept the sky clear of clouds. Even the moon, stars, and the wind wanted to please Luka.

Golden shards of candlelight reflected off his beautiful face. Pierce pulled a chair out for her and placed her napkin across her lap. He served a light dinner. Beef tips with egg noodles, with sautéed carrots and small boiled potatoes. Holly presented enough enthusiasm to forge an appetite and nibbled at the attractively designed portions. Luka instructed Pierce to put on an unusual CD selection, a Vegas crooner from the fifties. But the old crooner had been singing about love for decades, and he complimented the classic dinner setting and trance-like atmosphere perfectly.

After a few bites of an exquisitely delicious, chocolate soufflé, Luka offered his hand to dance. Everything about him was drawing her to him like that damned moth to the flame. She noticed the way his nose turned up at the tip or was it those impossible full, succulent lips that begged for constant kissing.

Here she stood again, comfortably wrapped in Luka's arms, well not that comfortable. Her body molded to his as naturally as salt, to sea air. He'd become her closest friend, confidant, and with any luck tonight, her lover. All she knew was she never wanted to leave him. His swaying body screamed one clear message, touch me and love me.

Locked safely in Luka's warm, comfortable embrace, under the spell of the enchanting moon, Holly exhaled a relaxing breath. She snuggled in closer, slipping her arms from his neck down inside his coat, over his shirt. She held him tighter, welcoming Luka's warm, loving hands as they surrounded her, his fingertips lightly stroking her bare back, coaxing her love to him.

Luka placed his ear next to the side of her face, rolled his head, and placed his lips on the side of her head, as he swayed to the magical music.

The scent of him lured her deeper into his male mystic. Occasionally, he dropped his lips onto her shoulder and marked a light trail of kisses, leaving her skin to be assaulted by the cool, moist sea air. He continued up and moved to the shell of her ear, tracing the rim with his lips and then the tip of his tongue. The tingling waves of hot, oh so hot thoughts, ravished her tired body. Yes, this was Luka. He was bringing her back to life, loving her, revitalizing her worn spirit, telling her with his body, she was safe with a promising future with him.

Luka's moist lips traced a tender trail along the long column of her neck to her chin, to spill over and reclaim her lips. He stopped, her eyes lifted to meet his. They locked; her stomach quivered. She knew he was reading her thoughts of wanting to love him. Her breath becoming uneven like it always did whenever this near him. And a sweet rush washed over her as his lips pressed against hers. The coolness of his lips deliciously, refreshing. His breath grew rough as the scent of him washed over her.

Mmmm, the sweet scent of him.

How delicious he was, like rich chocolate melting in her mouth. She moved closer to the scent of love. The air had tickled her ear before his words reached her.

"Happy Birthday, Babe."

She looked up to his beautiful, sunny smile, lost in the trance, blinded as usual.

"How beautiful you are Luka Hunter," she declared aloud, proud of her courage to tell him what she saw when she looked at him. With each seductive look, he grew more handsome, more desirable. The world vanished. All she saw — her beautiful angel. Nothing else existed — but him.

Oh, Luka.

When she sought a small breath of air to sustain her, the warmth and glow of his wonderful smile met her lusty gaze as if to confirm she was the most beautiful woman in the world.

He was a perfect dream.

How deeply she treasured him and the moment arrived to concentrate on kissing him. His breath grew rougher, as he kissed her deeper, slower, arousing her more, his tongue metering its arrival in her mouth, kissing her, placing his mouth first one way and then the other.

This was Luka.

It was too soon when Luka started to wean her purposefully from his powerful kisses. Never, had he shared this much of himself. And since he had, she clung to him helplessly like foam floating on the sea. She wanted to remain in the satiny depths of his never-ending love. To be lost in Neverland was always better. But he wasn't the fairy tale. He was real.

Luka continued kissing her lips until he needed to catch his breath. He moved, kissing her cheek, her ear until he hit upon her diamond stud earring.

His lips nudged it.

She snapped.

He hadn't realized.

He'd done the unforgivable!

He'd reminded her of Kaine giving her the diamond stud in London hours before the fight at Friar Manor. Everything about that dreadful fight flowed back at breakneck speed. How they'd fight over her being in Luka's arms, kissing him, as the hard lash of shame condemned her. This was no way for the mother of Kaine's child to behave and should put a stop to this

— but it would be hard.

Holly ran her hands along the firm curve of his back and placed her cheek against his chest. She grabbed for a sobering breath while her conscience desperately tried to prompt her to fight her way back to Kaine. But her body had long since betrayed all loyalties to Kaine. Her body claimed Luka the victor, to keep for herself alone. Reminding her of the possibilities to be happy with him if she gave him an equal chance.

But she couldn't. Because she knew, Luka would make her forget. She pulled away, letting her arm slide down his back as if all her dreams evaporated.

Luka's fingertips held her close, pressing into her back, holding her tighter than necessary. He was telling her, he understood the war going on inside her. He slipped his warm, smooth cheek against hers. He whistled lightly while he swayed with her to the intoxicating music.

Then he whispered.

"No pressure Babe, let me hold you.

"Close your eyes, forget everything but this moment."

Chapter Twenty-One

EVERY BREATH YOU TAKE

Impossible to do! Holly squeezed her eyes closed, hoping she would never leave this paradise. Surely, this was it! To be locked in Luka's arms?

It was impossible for Holly to control the weakness that rushed into her body as Luka's passionate kisses had scattered her emotions to the ends of the four winds.

Alone with Luka, too sensual, and she drew another shaky breath, as Luka held her close to him. She pressed her chest against his heart, following the beat, in rhythm with the old crooner vocals softly in the background. Suddenly, a chill filled the air, and Holly shivered as she watched the twinkling skyline of Santa Barbara grow closer. Too late!

Luka decided it was time to return home to the canyon.

Little over an hour later, Holly sat in Luka's Corvette crossing over Mulholland Drive, minutes from home. The quiet drive along the winding road gave her more time than she wanted to wonder about how quiet he'd been since the Day Dreamer.

Was Luka wondering what was going to happen between

them?

When and where would it happen?

How long could he keep himself from making love to her?

Too many questions, as usual, not enough answers. She stared at him. Incredibly sweet Luka, incredibly selfless, offering to father another man's child. And Kaine's no less!

The warnings from everyone crept into her thoughts like a thief again, shaking her trust in her own judgment. But worse, it made her suspect his real motives. How could she be in danger from Luka? All he did was show her a thousand different ways that he cared for her.

Luka showed her a spectacular birthday evening, filled with wonderful, romantic memories. And he'd single-handedly made her queen. It was too bad that the dear people in the *Hurrikaine* camp didn't see this new Luka Hunter. He'd certainly changed from their scathing descriptions of his past behavior. And why was everyone afraid of him, but her? She suddenly noticed what was strikingly different. How had she missed the obvious?

"Luka! I haven't seen you on the phone since we left the studio."

"You sound amazed?"

"That damn phone has ruined more plans I've spun concerning you."

Luka laughed a joyous Luka laugh.

"I don't have the phone tonight because I told Michael to handle my calls. That's why he's paid the big bucks."

She laughed, relieved, glad to release the heavy doubts that crushed her.

"If you have plans for me tonight," he offered lightly.

"I'm not expected to be on call until the morning."

He smiled letting her read his comment anyway she wanted. He threw her a playful wink as he parked behind her house.

Thankfully, no reporters perched there to define the moment for the world. She was hesitant. If she asked him in, she wasn't sure what to commit to, or what she'd be able to live with in the future.

Compelled to break the silence, she asked, "Coming inside, Luka?" Her query smooth, hoping he would, and hoping he wouldn't. Somehow, she knew if he said no, she would never ask him again.

Luka looked at her with many questions flooding his eyes.

She didn't have an answer for any of them. Only he held the answer.

"Well ... perhaps, for a little while."

The perfect answer.

She opened a couple of sparkling juices, poured them into stemware, and then joined him on the carpet, leaning across two of her giant pillows.

"I know little about you Luka, the basic things, like where do you call home?"

He laughed, "Well, you've been to the beach house. I also have a place in the hills to stay when I'm too tired to drive to the beach. A bachelor pad, I think it's called. I'm furnishing it. When it's done, you'll be my first guest for dinner."

Luka's British manners perfect, with no hint of impropriety.

"That would be nice. I'm looking forward to seeing how

you live."

"Nothing special."

"Like your BOAT!"

"Okay," he laughed heartily. "You bloody got me."

"What about your family?"

"There's me mum, and she flits about in Europe. *Hurrikaine's* been my family for the last twelve years. Guess they took it hard, me leaving considering the repercussions. I'm surprised to say, I did."

Possibly this was why everyone warned her? They thought Luka betrayed them when he left for CMT. Their experience tells them he will do the same to her. Or, possibly they're plain jealous of his good fortune without them? Stranger things had happened.

"Do you miss them a lot?" She'd decided to venture.

"Like anyone does that leaves home. You miss people that know you, can anticipate your needs. But it's even better to have a fresh start, as with you. I don't have to carry around old baggage and guilt and be consistently punished for things I've done. Maybe one day all their hard feelings will vanish, and we can all be a family again."

Those were the last words she'd expected from Luka, to be aware of the venom the *Hurrikaine* camp hurled toward him.

"You admit you see their animosity."

"Sure! I have feelings, Babe. Deep feelings when it comes to family. Don't you feel them from me? None of them are trying to hide their disapproval of me."

And how! She wanted to say. Instead, she calmed the shaking in her voice.

"There does seem to be an enormous strain between you and Kaine, beginning long before I showed up to muddy the waters. Unfortunately, everyone has sided with him. What is the problem? What do they think you've done that is unforgivable?"

Luka drained the juice.

"Nothing to bother your beautiful head about, it's in my past, and I'm getting on with my life at CMT. And hopefully, build something incredible with you."

Holly relished the special glow that only Luka stirred in her. The pale moonlight peeked in the window of her tiny cottage and wove in and out of his golden hair. He was too irresistible.

"Don't look at me with those eyes, Babe."

"What eyes?" She coyly whispered.

"Eyes that are filled with gratitude, but not...."

"These are the eyes of a woman who adores the man sitting next to her. Adores a man that she respects because he has selflessly given of himself, again and again, asking nothing in return."

Luka groaned and threw his head back, running two of his fingers through his hair hard and broke free the band holding back his hair. The golden strands tumbled down all around to touch his shoulders.

Her mouth ran dry. It was her turn to groan. She threaded her fingers in a long lock of his hair and pulled herself closer to him.

He groaned too.

Holly moved closer. She followed the edge of his jawline, to his perfect lips begging her to kiss them. Perhaps this was it. She'd never dreamed it would be her seducing him. And oh, how she wanted to suck on his full, ripe lips with complete abandon. She ran her tongue over her lips, wetting them, and moved even closer. She looked Luka straight in the eyes and then grabbed a ragged breath to give herself the courage to follow her thoughts and desires.

His face, inspirational — beautiful. Then he closed his blue eyes to-die-for.

She whispered, "Let me convince you to stay with me tonight."

A groan clogged in his chest, breaking the silence. He opened his dreamy eyes.

"Don't ask me to, Babe. I'm trying to do this right, and you're always making it damn difficult." His hair fell as he shook his head from side-to-side.

She'd never seen a more beautiful angel man, ever. Then she laughed.

"Me difficult? What is it you want to do right? We are right! You've told me many ways, and I'm saying, I agree. There I've said it. Let me show you how wonderful, and special you are to me."

Instead of Luka rushing her as she'd hoped, he looked away as if afraid, unsure, that if he looked at her again, he wouldn't be able to stop her.

He moved away and stood. "No, especially not tonight Babe."

His face wore an expression she didn't understand. He sat shaking. It was difficult for her to understand that Luka would be vulnerable, and when he spoke, he surprised her even more.

"If I wanted sex from you, I could have slept with you

any of those nights in London. I should have, our first night, and none of this would have happened with Kaine. Bloody Hell, I don't know. What I do know. I don't want you lying beside me until you are sure you're finished with Kaine and not mesmerized with me, or an evening out."

She was thunderstruck by his attitude.

"Luka, how can you say that? You make my feelings for you sound superficial, dirty."

He smiled the boyish grin she'd come to adore, and the corners of his mouth pushed up a single dimple.

"I didn't say that proper. Trust, that's what I want from you. I want you to realize I'm not Kaine. I'm not going to wine and dine you, create the perfect evening, and then as a nightcap have sex with you. You'll be waiting for me to abandon you like he did. No! This time, I'm doing it right."

"Do I get a say in this decision?"

"No!" He growled.

"What is it you want from me? You say you want my trust. Yet you act as if you're not only afraid to trust me, but yourself as well? You need more than trust?"

"I do ..." His voiced trailed.

She'd hit a wound. An old one by the way he reacted. She watched him decide if he did trust her enough to tell her.

"Try to trust me, Luka. Trust that I won't be so charmed by Kaine I'd leave you ...."

She'd almost said *again*.

"Yes, it's true. I think the same thing. You might leave me *again*. You politely omitted that word. I'll tell you exactly what I want. I want a relationship. And without trust, there can be no relationship. Yes, I realize it's not what you would expect from a man in my position. I tried to explain this to you in London. I am a man that is looking not only sex but for a commitment. I've traveled this world enough times to learn the highs of lust with sex don't last long. I want my feelings for you to last forever. I can only hope after you get Kaine Walker out of your system, I'll have proven to you, I'm different."

"Luka, my darling man, you've proved that already. Look at what we have overcome?"

"True, but you're not facing the realities of a relationship with me."

"I have!"

"First, I don't want your damned gratitude. What I want, you won't give me. Are you ready to say, 'I'll marry you, Luka, you father my child?' Are you prepared to make a commitment like that with me?"

Holly sat dumbfounded. No words would come. Luka never hinted at his desire to marry her. And if he wouldn't have hidden behind his words, and put the proposal to her straight, at another time and place, she might have said the powerful words.

Yes, I'll marry you.

But he hadn't.

And she couldn't.

She remained silent.

"As I thought, Kaine stands between us. And I do understand. You just found out you're carrying his child. I can't imagine how that news changes your future. But I care too much to get intimately involved with you, only to have Kaine waltz back into your life and take you away from me ...

a second time. You want a confession. Then think about this. I want to roll over when I'm old and have you be the first beautiful vision I see each morning."

Hot, stinging tears sprang to well in her eyes because her heart was breaking. And when did she become a woman with no integrity, trying to seduce this wonderful man while she carried another man's child? The shame bit at her heart, and before she looked away, she locked onto his eyes that turned a stormy blue. They announced his passion was suspended but a breath away from erupting. She closed her eyes for a moment to center her as an overwhelming confusion swept over her.

"Luka, forgive me for what am I doing to you."

"Nothing I can't handle. But one day, and understand, I speak the truth. I will make love to you. I'm tired of cold showers and this hot fire in my gut for you. I've learned a lot of tricks traveling around the world, but when I'm with you, I want our real feelings. I don't want us running from our past, good or bad. I want to share my love with you when we are together and show you ways of pleasure you've never imagined. Mostly, I want to hear MY name on your lips, Holly. Not Kaine's."

Holly shivered, unable to stop her body. She was crushed. She remembered how she'd spoken Kaine's name when Luka was about to enter her body. Her insides twisted into an ugly black knot. She stepped closer to him, but he stepped back.

She whispered, "Please, don't."

Her hand instantly went up to his face. She bent her finger and traced the outline of his lips.

"Someone once told me I didn't deserve you, and I finally understand tonight that they were right."

She leaned back and her hands moved swiftly to the top of his waistband. She located the metal zipper and pulled downwards. She was going as far as he would let her.

"Yes, you do," he replied after a moment of indecision and added a long ragged sigh.

Luka dropped his hand on her wrist and pulled her hand away from him as he groaned. He placed it on his cheek. He forced a smile, the usual sunny smile, so obligatory, so unnatural.

He offered no more advice or wisdom. He released her and stepped back away from her then headed for the door.

Holly ambled toward him as if struck and the blow left her dizzy.

"Is there anything I can say to change your mind?"

"Yes. But you're not ready to say those words to me."

Luka reached out quickly, surprising her by grabbing her by the waist with one arm, and pulling her into his sweet embrace.

Holly watched him quickly suck in his bottom lip because she hit his heart.

Luka leaned dangerously close to her face, he whispered.

"Happy Birthday, Babe. I have one last surprise for you. Keep the diamonds and the dress as presents from me."

"But Luka!"

He shut her up with a kiss. Not any kiss. The kiss that awakened her making her realize that Luka Hunter wasn't ever going to leave her.

Then her mind whirled on to the diamonds, worth hundreds of thousands of dollars. The gown, an Asset original! Together worth a small fortune. Should she continue to protest? She wanted the gifts from him. Deep in her heart, she was grateful.

Luka leaned back a breath away from her face, mixing his breath with hers.

"Enjoy yourself," and then he delivered another birthday wish in a breathy voice.

"Happy birthday, my beauty," as he squeezed her tightly against him.

His body responded to her.

He quickly let go of her.

He opened the door and vanished into the fog.

Chapter Twenty-Two

WALTZING BACK

Waves of disappointment wouldn't stop. Holly listened for Luka's car to start. Hot tears trickled down her cheeks, mourning what might have been between them. Then her thoughts strayed to practical matters. To suitable security, maybe a personal safe, or a bank deposit box for the necklace.

Life in the fast lane and things were changing again.

Holly looked down and noticed a box leaning out of the way, behind a bush near the doorway. When she lifted the lid, the contents revealed a dozen red roses. The card read.

Thinking of you on your birthday.
I wish I could have celebrated with you.
Love, Brett.

Holly took the flowers and placed them in a large vase. She looked over at the clock, it read midnight. It should have been a magical time with Luka. Why was it with Luka and Kaine, the exquisite pleasure was always followed by excruciating pain? This time, the pain was Luka's. She'd seen the hurt and rejection in his eyes because she wasn't ready to commit. Why did he have to ask if she was willing to marry him and allow him to be declared the father of Kaine's child? That wasn't her future.

Too upset to sleep, Holly slipped into a vanilla scented tub topped with creamy bubbles. It hadn't been too long when the phone rang and being so late, she let the machine answer. Perhaps it was Luka speeding back toward her, unable to stay away. He'd done that the last night in London.

She heard the soft British accent.

"Holly? It's Emily. I see I've called while you are out. I get confused with the time changes. I'll ..."

Holly picked up her cordless phone before she could finish her sentence.

"Emily? Is everything okay?"

They both understood what she asked.

"I wish I had good news for you. Things are quickly deteriorating here in Rome."

"Rome, how romantic."

"Well, yes, for a few people. But for us, thankfully, Rome is the end of this leg of the tour. The band performed their final concert night before last. And since Kaine and Ian have been in studio laying down tracks."

"I've heard." And she quickly brought Emily up to speed.

"You are well-informed, considering we're half way around the world. But I'm calling with the latest."

"I'd hoped nothing worse would happen."

"There's no way to say this without alarming you. It's a well-guarded secret. Kaine's in hospital here in Rome. He was found alone, collapsed in the studio. The medical team says its exhaustion mixed with malnourishment due to his continual mistreatment of his body. They say he's abusing cocaine. None of us knows where he's been getting the drugs since Luka left. He's in a bad way, and the clinic's started detoxing Kaine. In forty-eight hours, Kaine will be transferred to a specialist in substance abuse. And because of a possible leak to the press, I'm sworn to secrecy exactly where he's being sent."

"Oh Emily, I'm glad to hear he'll get the help he needs. I'm sure everyone connected with the tour is relieved Kaine finished the European tour."

"Yes, it's a miracle. The tour is officially over, and since the management company planned to add dates along the way, the press statement will read — no additional dates added due to a virus. That's what they're calling Kaine's rapidly deteriorating condition. Remember, if anyone questions you, especially Luka, Kaine contracted a severe virus."

"Is there anything I can do Emily," Holly offered, hoping the irrational thoughts would vanish that she was responsible for this latest turn of events.

"Not anything you're willing to do," she stated as if to let the sword pierce Holly anyway it could.

"I'll be accompanying Kaine, and Nicky is coming with us. The rest of the band is heading out to the states tonight to stay with their families for the holidays. It's not a surprise to the band that the tour finished with no new dates. As you mentioned, they're relieved Kaine made it to the end. But Kaine would, millions of dollars were riding on him, and Kaine is a performer first, a businessman second. But no matter, the experience was unnerving. The last two months he's bloody well been dancing with the demons of Hell."

"You mean because of me," Holly whispered, her words laced with shame, believing her betrayal to be the single cause of Kaine's demise.

Emily, always quick in her reply.

"No, that's rubbish! You mustn't think that! Kaine has battled his addictions long before you. He knew better than to play with fire. The last substance abuse specialist warned him that if he started drugs again, he would pick up right where he'd left off, and he certainly has done that. It's essential that Kaine accepts in his bloody, thick head, once and for all, any mind altering substances are poison to him. What's the saying 'one's too many and a thousand not enough? That's the way it is with Kaine.

"While I agree, you were an influential variable in this complicated equation, it's Kaine's addiction and unwillingness to look at himself and face his problems that has ultimately caused the pair of you much pain and grief."

Holly forced a winded response.

"I thought the root of his problems stemmed from the ghost of Briarwood?"

"You're right, of course. Briarwood is the root cause of his unresolved trauma's that prompted him to drown his secrets and pain in drugs in the first place. He's never been able to acknowledge it in the past, and I'm sure his choice of careers contributed.

"Music helped him to run away, keeping him looking outward, instead of inward, keeping the ghost at the bottom of Kaine's self-destructive pyramid. And once he's met this demon straight on and faced him, then and only then, can he rebuild a healthy life on solid ground, and live a healthy, happy life with you.

"I know this because I've dealt with the same issues of Father's controlling nature and his limitless abuse and brutality. One of these days when we have time, I will tell you more about Briarwood and father. But I'm needed. I have to get back to Nicky and oversee the packing for our departure. I won't be able to call often. Give me your fax number. I may be out of touch for as long as thirty days."

Holly gave her the information and added, "Thirty days?"

"That's the minimum stay for drug rehabilitation. We hope Kaine will be strong enough to attend the wedding. Since we're keeping this explosive news from the press, and you're being watched so closely, I'll get in touch when I can, with updates on how my brother is doing."

"Emily, I do appreciate your calls."

Holly quietly thought of the wedding. He had to be well enough to attend. And though the lash of selfishness hit hard, she knew in her heart, if he didn't, she might never see him again. She'd never be able to share with him the joy and incredible news.

He was a father.

She dropped her head in shame and frustration.

"I need to be in Rome to help Kaine."

"Yes, you do. You would be the best medicine, you, and his child. Kaine was there for me each step of the way during my breakdown and then recovery. We're exceptionally close, and there's nowhere I'd rather be than beside him. However, Kaine's first steps to healing are to enter into treatment to make a future possible for the pair of you. We both know he loves you, Holly.

"And that's another thing that's eating at him. He's much more sensitive than he'd like to let on, and his love for Luka is evolving into hatred because of the betrayal."

Holly's stomach knotted squeezing her guilt.

"Emily, I'm a terrible mess. I do love him so. Day after day, our baby grows stronger. I find myself dreaming of a wonderful future together."

"Keep your dreams of a family with Kaine. Realize that I've delivered frightening words. Alcohol, cocaine, treatment center, abusing his body, and you continue to love him and don't want to run away. Your love is genuine for my brother. Holly, hold on to your belief that it can happen. You may get your miracle. I've got to ring off ... sorry."

Emily's words of encouragement hung fragrantly in the air.

Hold on to your belief it can happen.

The inspirational words circled in Holly's head. Eventually, they settled in her heart as she lay picturing her lover in a Rome hospital bed, depressed and unhappy. And how horrible that she wasn't there to hold his hand, soothe and comfort him.

However, this news didn't devastate her and caused her to cry. Perhaps the worst was over for her, but the worst yet to come for Kaine.

Holly got up and for the first time, it looked like she might be able to get over her self-loathing and betrayal with Luka and face Kaine ... that a glimmer of hope existed.

She put on a clean *Hurrikaine* T-shirt, with the name of the tour on the front *Lost Dreams ... Lost Illusions.* She slipped into his band jacket and his soothing scent. Then she popped the cassette cartridge into the mouth of her VCR. She brought home a clean copy of CMT's latest exclusive of Kaine in the studio singing "My Lady."

Holly fell asleep with Kaine's voice singing her song, her love for him safely locked in her heart.

It was a happy birthday.

Chapter Twenty-Three

JUST REMEMBER
I LOVE YOU

Three long weeks passed, and work at CMT moved fast, the pace exciting. Halloween came and went. There was silence from the *Hurrikaine* camp. Luka kept a professional distance filling her in on the details of all his business deals in progress. And that was fine with her.

That night, her dreams filled with a thick mist and shadows. A figure moved, waiting at the edge. She barely saw the face blocked by a circling mist. She closed her eyes. He lifted the blanket, and the bed depresses beside her. His body slipped in, bringing the warmth of his to cover hers. His hand slid smoothly. He stopped and placed his hand gently on the place where she carried the miracle of love.

He moved closer, fitting his body in line with hers. She allowed her hand the joyful trip running up his strong arm. His hand moved on around her waist and pulled her into his firm body. Warm, alive, and he pressed her harder. His mouth found her neck and dropped a trail of kisses up over her chin.

When he arrived at her waiting lips, his mouth closed over hers, sweetly, and gently, telling her he loved her, forever.

He reminded her to trust his one of a kind forever love that bound them together across time and distance. Then he pulled away from her lips that sought more of his sweet, sweet kisses.

He moved his mouth to her ear. He started to sing his love to her. The "My Lady" lyrics spilled softly. At first, she barely heard them. He whispered the words as his arms pulled her tighter, his body, loving her, moving in closer, as if he intended to climb inside her body, to share the one skin of their love.

She whispered, "I love you."

When he finished singing the last lyric, he whispered in her ear.

"I love you too My Lady, three and four times, a million times...."

She moved to close her arms around him. She moved to pull him in close ... but nothing was there, only mist and shadows.

The next morning she woke up with tears in her eyes. Her dream lover left her with his strong presence. She lay empty, alone and cold.

Holly crawled out of bed, tired, drained, and as usual, followed by the expected nausea. Her thoughts drifted to the dream as she tried to swallow bits of cracker. Like so many dreams of Kaine she'd experienced lately — this one had been too real.

Powerful, as if she truly touched him, kissed him, enjoyed the pleasure of him as if one body. Sadness engulfed her, sorrow for her sweet Kaine, reduced to becoming her dream lover, scarcely able to come to her by darkness.

Holly rose with one thought, Kaine.

She sipped hot black tea and planning her day. Today was as good as any to start her investigation into the Briarwood incident. She dressed in a pair of black leggings, shimmied into a black lace, three-quarter length, vintage dress she'd bought on trendy Melrose Avenue and knee-high black boots.

When Holly arrived at her desk, a message waited, instructing her to go straight to Michael's office.

Oh no!

Not another meeting with Michael. Anxiety riddled her. Each visit to Michael's office proved life altering. First this incredible job opportunity, then Kaine in the recording studio, and next the "My Lady" video shoot.

Holly briskly walked down the long corridor heading toward Michaels. She reasoned it must have something to do with the video shoot. They needed to shoot more footage, but that was silly. That was Luka's decision as the producer, and since she hadn't heard from him that day, she guessed there was no need to shoot more footage today.

She hurried up to Michael's secretary and was ushered into the office where she found Michael sitting, impeccably dressed in a charcoal colored, pinstriped Asset suit.

Luka stood nearby casually dressed in a crisp sky-blue, button-down Brooks Bros. shirt, making his dreamy blue eyes sparkle even brighter and cuffed khaki's, sockless, with his cinnamon-colored Gucci loafers.

She sat waiting to find out why she had been summoned.

Michael started innocently enough.

"Holly, we have the footage edited, and I'd like to show it to you."

Luka walked over to the enormous TV usually hidden in a bookcase and pushed a button. Magically a giant-sized image of Holly filled the screen.

She sat frozen.

Holly watched herself, amazed at her own image. The magic of editing out-takes from the first video "Now That I've Found You," had the frames painstakingly spliced together creating her and Kaine again on celluloid, twisted into each other's arms again.

"As you can imagine Holly, we are tremendously pleased with the results of this product. This brings up another project Luka is producing. A new interview show scheduled to run twenty-two minutes. CMT will run it on a six-hour rotation slot. The premise is a candid look at the life of a different chart-topping performer each week.

"We've interviewed candidates to host it for months with no success. Luka noticed the day you arrived in London and faxed me that night demanding you take the spot on "Now That I've Found You."

"Frank edited the video with Luka, and they thought you'd be a natural. I trusted Luka's instincts and agreed. As you can see, he was spot-on.

"We have talked it over, we agree, you're exactly what we want for this project. It's clear that you have the talent, and it's worth mentioning your cultic following around the world, as the *Hurrikaine's* mystery lady will help to provide a built-in audience. I was pleasantly surprised to learn that you worked on the Collins murder trial, and that lends us an extra audience, and that's a definite plus for CMT.

"However, what counts most is the camera. And Holly, it adores you. Coupled with all your recent global headlines with Luka, we agree you're the only candidate to become the host."

Holly reached down for the arm of the chair again. She descended into the chair dumbstruck and flattered both at once.

Michael took a sharp breath and continued.

"Holly, we're offering you a top of the line job with a competitive salary package, quality benefits, company car of your choice, and clothing allowance. That way we assumed you would choose your own costumes, and bring your own personal touch to the show. Since Luka's the producer of the show, you would work directly with him.

"I'm going to turn this project to him. There are lunch reservations to run over the details and his thoughts on how the pilot show will be shot. He has the information, set location, and first month's guest list. Buckle your seat belt, Holly. You're in the fast lane. Luka's will make you a star!"

Her future, a matter of fact.

They presumed she wouldn't refuse this offer. Was this what Luka had up his sleeve all the time?

To make her a star?

She heard Kaine saying.

You will find out that what I think is of little use.

I am to sell tickets and records.

He is my personal manager/producer.

Michael leaned forward, lacing his fingers, waiting for her response. She knew better than to wait, this was the offer of a lifetime. Her own television show! Who would have predicted that she could pull off a TV show?

Luka, of course, always far ahead of her.

This was what everyone warning her about because Luka didn't do anything without a reason. He'd spotted her as a possible candidate for his new show when he caught her from falling on that Chelsea Street. He'd kept her close, grooming her, waiting for the right time to spring his trap. Of course, he'd get his way, and she would have her own show, be her own boss. Well, almost, she would answer to Luka.

I am the pawn for him to move about.

Holly remembered Kaine's words and realized she would never be her own boss.

She looked up at him.

Luka's face never revealed his thoughts. He was doing it again, forcing her to stand on her own two feet, to make the decision without his influence. He'd made his stand, putting her on notice. If she wanted, she could pass on the opportunity.

Holly looked at Michael, then to Luka. She took a small breath to assist her struggle to keep her voice calm and even, to be the professional they'd expected to hire, and she answered.

"Naturally, I'm overwhelmed, Michael, Luka, and I'm flattered by your confidence to offer me the important position at CMT to host the new project. Of course, I accept and look forward to familiarizing myself with the pilot. You can count on me to do my best work for you."

She sat back and then added. "By the way, what's the title of the show?"

Michael smiled a devious smile. "Not *the* show, *your*

show Holly. It's your show. We were discussing it before you arrived. What are your thoughts on, "The Heart of Holly Would?" You see, the twist on words."

Holly never saw the traffic or heard the CD playing in Luka's car as he drove her to lunch in Beverly Hills. Lost in a whirlwind of thoughts Holly's mind was scrambled as if she'd stepped off a twisted roller coaster.

When Luka finished sharing the six test show ideas with her, he suddenly asked her out-of-the-blue.

"Have you received the latest news about the *Hurrikaine* tour?"

The curse of defensiveness attacked her, and she didn't want to skirt the issue and lie to Luka. Especially, after all, he had done for her.

She cautiously ventured. "I assume you mean the fact that it has finished?"

"Yes, exactly! Who told you?"

"Emily called." And remembering Emily's strong warning. "Kaine is ill with a foreign virus, I understand?"

"Yes, that's what I was told too, but I wonder."

Holly watched suspicions spread in his eyes. To protect her friends so far away, she quickly changed the subject.

"What are your plans for Thanksgiving? Do you celebrate this American holiday?"

"No, not before *Hurrikaine,* a conflict of interest, but I admit, I've rather grown fond of turkey dinner with the trimmings, as a result of *Hurrikaine* being Americans. I've been invited to go with Michael and his family to Sheridan, Wyoming. And you? Home to Santa Barbara?"

"Not sure. My parents left a message that they are flying

back east to visit my mom's sister."

"Well then, why don't you come along with us to Sheridan? I understand Michael has a beautiful home tucked away at the foot of the Big Horn Mountain with a spectacular view. If you ski, I'm told the skiing this time of year is great. I can promise we'll be relaxing. It could give you and I a chance to put the past behind us and focus on a bright future. You fancy the idea?"

Her thoughts spun, wondering how to get out of this predicament and dare to say no, but not offend Luka. She wasn't quite up for being a cheerful companion or courteous guest, not even for Luka. She wanted time alone to sort her life out since too much happened in too short of time. Going on vacation with Luka would certainly confuse her more. She couldn't take another rejection from him, even if he were trying to 'do it right'. At this point, she wanted to hide in the canyon and decide her own fate.

"Thanks, Luka, but I'm not fishing for an invitation. I'll find something to do."

"Rubbish, you're coming with us to Sheridan. I insist. Do you have any warm clothing?"

Holly allowed a small laugh, knowing she'd never win this round by the confident look in Luka's eyes.

She explained. "I'm a native Californian, Luka. I have nothing to protect me from the real cold."

"That's it! We're going shopping."

"I can't!"

"Yes, you can. But if you insist, I'll take it out of your clothing allowance. Miss Hill, we're going shopping."

They hit all the designer shops along the world famous

Rodeo Drive and the unusual boutiques on the surrounding streets until little room existed in Luka's tiny convertible for any more purchases.

Later that evening tucked away at home in the canyon, Holly lit the stacked logs in her fireplace. She sat back contemplating how different her world turn out to be since last Thanksgiving. There's been little time for celebrating with the Collins murder trial in full swing.

Long after Luka left, she hung up the last of her dream purchases, mulling over why he hadn't kissed her goodbye.

Were those days gone?

Was he being honorable and keeping his distance?

Some moments she was glad, but others miserable. She pulled out the Louis Vuitton KeepAll and remembered that Kaine sent it to her along with the things she acquired in London.

Luka insisted she buys matching pieces of Louis Vuitton luggage to complete a set. He'd put them on her expense account, assuring her she would eventually travel due to "Heart of Holly Would," or 'HHW' as he called the show.

Long after midnight, Holly lay restless in her bed, thinking. She traveled in the fast lane and needed to stop to assimilate the new information. Another twenty-four hours passed, and she'd amassed a long list of new happenings piling up becoming an avalanche of changes.

As she drifted to sleep, her last thoughts centered on positive thoughts for Kaine to keep his strength up for the ordeal he faced in the rehabilitation clinic. That was the one chance they had for a future if he managed his addiction. Otherwise, how could she commit to a globe-trotting, drug addict and expect to have a healthy relationship and raise a family? Yes, Kaine would have to draw on his inner strength and courage to help him succeed during the next crucial weeks.

The next day, Holly busied herself with her first production meeting to introduce her to the principals involved with her show. Wow, HER show! What an incredible sound that had. After the brief meeting, she'd dashed home to pack … then on to meet Luka and Michaels' family at the Burbank Airport, to board the CMT jet, destination Sheridan, Wyoming.

Upon arrival at the airport, Holly was respectively intimidated by Michael and his overwhelming impact on her life. After all, he and Luka single-handedly created and reshaped her future forever. And they were changing her circle of intimate friends.

Yes, here she was, ready to take part in a cherished family holiday such as Thanksgiving. But to spend it with an almost, total stranger, and the COO of the company she that employed her, with his family, was a bit much.

Holly hoped she would remain calm and not make a fool of herself. However, her anxiety quickly melted. There stood Michael, comfortably dressed in red, wool, ski sweater, light blue Levi's, and white, high-top athletic shoes, looking like an ordinary traveler. Well, except for the corny red ski hat that amused her. No one would have ever suspected that Michael was a self-made multi-millionaire.

Michael's lovely wife Catherine was as sweet as she was beautiful. Catherine, easily over forty, well taken care of, was lean and athletically toned. Her shoulder-length, straight blonde hair, was blunt cut. Her face was make-up free, with huge jade-green eyes and a warm, gracious smile and dressed casually in a persimmon colored jogging suit. She put Holly at ease at once.

Their seventeen-year-old son Keith was dark-haired and as wholesomely handsome as his father. Crissy, their beautiful daughter, was fifteen, and a spitting image of her mother, only her hair touched her waist. They seemed to be genuinely happy and loving toward each other and reminded her of home.

Perhaps Thanksgiving will be a happier time.

She had much to be thankful for, most of all, the precious gift she carried.

Chapter Twenty-Four

SUGAR BABE

The four-hour flight to Sheridan, Wyoming, was marvelous. Holly sat at ease with Luka, playing video games. Michael turned out to be a gracious host, and his welcoming family took her into their hearts. After the ten-hour flight from London, she'd grown used to the private CMT jet, with its luxurious accommodations providing ultra-comfort. The only way to travel and she enjoyed being indulged and pampered no longer needed to cope with any of the customary congestion and confusion of commercial flights — especially during Thanksgiving with airports a nightmare.

The CMT jet landed in the tiny Sheridan airport, and Michael drove them for miles along snow-dusted, back roads in a black Land Rover left for him at the airport by his caretaker. Michael, inspired by the beauty of the landscape, sang comfortably along with the CD playing, as he headed for his snowbound hide away.

Holly smiled as the exhilaration took hold while passing tall, snow-brushed evergreen trees, waiting to be cut and adopted, to delight families for weeks at Christmas time.

Crissy cracked the window, and the crisp, cool air, gushed in saturated with the thick, refreshing scent of pine. Michael continued to drive up a hill until they arrived at a gate. Crissy pointed to the summit of the upgrade, to a tiny dot in the sky, the family cabin.

Crissy smiled and started to speak to no one, in particular.

"This is the edge of our property. We also have a pond to the right and down the hill for ice skating in the winter and fishing in the summer. We have hundreds of acres for our cattle to roam. But we won't see any at this time of year because of the weather."

After a moment's pondering, she excitedly exclaimed.

"Holly, wait until you see Freedom Lodge!"

"Freedom Lodge?" Holly repeated with a tone of curiosity.

"Yes," Catherine interjected. "Please forgive Crissy for going on ungraciously. But as the story goes, this location is the first piece of real estate Michael purchased in the late sixties as a hideaway for temperamental musicians. He coined the phrase, 'we're hiding out at Freedom Lodge,' free of phones, T.V., and his demanding staff when he produced records for Spectacular Records."

The lodge stood quiet and magnificent, three stories high and looked more like a ski lodge than a privately owned log cabin. The rest of the landscape looked barren, covered with a thick, downy blanket of fresh snow.

Parked at the summit, Holly wandered about the outside of the breathtaking lodge. The sweeping panoramic view was like nothing she'd ever seen or imagined. The grandeur and splendor of the Big Horn Mountains, cloaked in a thick, white, winter coat, brought a fresh wave of tears to her eyes to honor nature's finest work. The century-old log cabin appeared appropriately rustic and comfortable with none of the finer trappings of Michael's apparent wealth.

Holly continued to stroll along the length of the ground floor porch that surrounded the lodge, awestruck by the astounding three hundred and sixty-degree cinematic views of the snow-covered valley.

She came upon Luka combing his hair with his fingers, equally awed by the grandeur of the Big Horn Mountain Range that stretched out lazily for as far as they could see. His other arm naturally snaked out and coiled around her waist, pulling her to him. There was no public eye from which to hide. Therefore, here, Luka could show her his tender feelings.

Luka held her close, and neither spoke. Nature's grace washed over them. The majestic view promised to lure her away to a secret place with Luka she may never want to leave.

Catherine served the dinner's main course, a simple family effort of roasted chicken dressed with canned and pickled vegetables, and other assorted dried fruits she'd retrieved from the cellar that she'd preserved on her last visit.

Later, the small group toasted marshmallows on sticks in front of the massive, frontier stone fireplace. They all sat hypnotized by the crackling fire in the mammoth hearth. The family sipped hot chocolate, until well past midnight, enjoying hours of board games.

During the board game, Michael casually commented.

"Holly, I'm glad you decided to join us. I'm happy to share this small piece of paradise with you, after all, you've been through lately."

She smiled graciously knowing her decadent reputation preceded her. She wondered how many details of her life had he been privy to, and she looked to Luka. He winked.

Later that night after everyone said good night, Holly settled into her cozy, upstairs guest suite. She loved the rustic, down-home environment, and Wyoming became a contender for another excellent place to raise her precious bundle — *Kaine's child.*

From nowhere melancholy took hold, causing her to wonder where she would bring her child into this world. She wandered around her winter wonderland, fantasy bedroom, complete with the obligatory four log-posts, canopied bed draped with a corduroy, and satin, patchwork quilt, of dark greens and browns and the soft mattress stuffed liberally with down feathers.

The roaring fire in the fireplace existed only served to complete the atmosphere of the log wall décor since the central heating kept her room warm and toasty. She discovered a small refrigerator, stocked with juices and mineral waters. An assortment of nuts, dried fruits, and individually wrapped chocolates sat conveniently placed on a wooden tray.

Holly looked out her floor-to-ceiling window exposing the Big Horn Mountains. How brightly they glowed because the silver moon's reflection sparkled on the glistening snow-capped mountains and valley. She put on her new, floor-length pink and white flannel nightgown and fell into a contented slumber. There she dreamed of Luka holding her. It had been a long time coming.

"DAMN IT!" Catherine squealed as she banged her finger

against the hot turkey broiler, and then quickly held the injured finger under cold water.

Holly was impressed she'd not hired a professional staff to prepare the Thanksgiving feast. She and Michael were a remarkably down-to-earth family. Catherine explained that Michael gave the caretaker the long holiday off to be home with his family.

Crissy sat in the corner, kneading dough for fresh baked bread. Holly whistled a gentle tune as she happily pitched in cutting celery for the stuffing, like one of the family. She occasionally peeked out the kitchen window that took up most of the wall, losing herself in the unusual scene unfolding before her. Luka frolicking in the light snowfall, throwing a football back and forth to Keith. In this lost and forgotten paradise, the sex roles reverted to the traditional style of women in the kitchen, men outside playing sports since there was no TV reception.

Catherine moved close and playfully bumped Holly with her hip and spoke.

"You watch Luka like a starved cat."

Holly whirled around quickly.

"Do I?" She quickly tried to cover the look of surprise.

"Since the first moment, I saw you lay eyes on him at the airport. Something a woman would see. Don't worry, you're not obvious," she replied and smiled coyly.

"Doesn't sound like it. A starved cat? Really?"

The words hung heavy in the air, and then both women burst out in a robust round of laughter.

"Well, a weak kitten, maybe. He is beautiful, no doubt of that."

Holly leaned back on the counter and sighed. Yes, that was the problem. He was such a looker. Even with snowflakes dusting his head and shoulders, there was nothing more beautiful than Luka Hunter laughing and enjoying himself. Well, perhaps one other time, when his eyes lit up and sparkled whenever he looked at her.

Catherine changed the subject fast.

"I've always prepared dinner with Crissy. It's wonderful to have you here with us this year."

Holly sensed Catherine wanted details, but Holly didn't have any. But she did recognize she couldn't imagine a day without Luka in her life any longer.

"How long have you known Luka?" Holly decided to make use of the moment.

"I met him about two years ago. Michael was courting him, hoping to lure Luka away from *Hurrikaine* to work at CMT."

"Michael recruited Luka? Do you know why Luka decided to leave *Hurrikaine*?"

"Michael likes to say he made Luka an offer even he couldn't refuse. It took a lot of dinners, trips, and private meetings. I didn't see Michael much for close to a year. He was desperate. CMT's ratings were trampled on by the other music station. Michael's last hope was Luka's business genius and being globally well connected. For many years, Luka was loyal to only the band. Then Michael realized he would lose CMT if he didn't give Luka what he wanted."

"That was?"

"Well, this info is not common knowledge, but seeing how you are becoming family. Stock in CMT. That apparently altered the tide."

"Luka owns shares of CMT?"

"He may own more shares than Michael, and he founded CMT. I guess it would be fair to say, Luka is Michael's boss."

Holly sensed that to be true, deep in her gut.

"You'll learn soon enough, not a day goes by they aren't involved making deals. They are two of a kind. And I don't mind sharing with you. Something's brewing. I recognize all the signs. Michael has his cellular phone on all the time. The fax machine is spitting paper like confetti. And, Michael's asked for privacy the last night of our trip. Usually means there's a secret meeting planned. This must be a big deal to require this much seclusion to close a deal."

She knew what Catherine spoke of, but what Catherine didn't know was that she was privy to Luka's private deals at CMT with both Michael as CEO and with Clive, CMT-UK's CEO, though he answered to Michael. Correction, both men, answered to Luka, as she did. The thought crossed her mind that Luka might be preparing her for a much larger position in the corporate structure of CMT's future.

Holly set the celery aside and moved to chop cranberries.

Catherine smiled, to show Holly, she welcomed Holly's skilled hand in the kitchen.

Holly kept her thoughts to herself, but noted it was time to keep a closer eye on Luka something was brewing.

The women's day started at seven, to prepare the turkey and all day long, the men flitted about checking the fax machine, taking occasional calls. Though it was Thanksgiving, Michael and Luka kept their heads together most of the time including games of Backgammon and Scrabble.

This was why Luka wanted her here. What Luka wanted her to see. How family life would function with him? He'd explained to her in London what marriage would be when men like him and Kaine, needed to balance family and empires.

Luka wanted her to see a success story. Michael and Catherine found the balance. This was how it would be married to Luka and raising children. He wanted her to see for herself that they could make it work. Thanksgiving at home with the Hunter's, the wealthy, and the powerful.

Thanksgivings at home in Santa Barbara were fond memories for Holly. She smiled, remembering her mother, working side-by-side in the kitchen, cooking for the legions of friends invited to the feast each year.

A tight grip squeezed a pain in her heart as Holly spent a moment missing her mom and dad. She silently thanked them for giving her the space she needed to find a way to explain the Malibu fiasco in the papers. She needed to figure out how to tell her parents about her impending pregnancy by a man, as far as they were concerned, a complete stranger.

They'd always respected her privacy and tried not to pry. But when would be a good time to tell them about their grandchild? Would there ever be the right moment?

They'd understood. There'd been no reproach when she called home with her explanation of the awful Malibu photos. Her father, a newspaper editor, too familiar with the rag paper business, would expect extenuating circumstances to prevail. And as much as she missed her parents, she was glad she'd agreed to accompany Luka, rather than stay in the canyon and soak in her tub.

Over the next few days, Michael and Catherine scheduled

fun activities. Holly and Luka beat Catherine and Michael in a snowball fight. How wonderful to go snowboarding, especially with Luka sitting behind her holding her tight. How peaceful and romantic when they went horseback riding along the lower trails in the snow-packed Big Horns. She never noticed she'd forgotten Kaine. The family visited the quaint one-street town of Sheridan, where everyone knew your first name and a stranger for a short time.

Saturday, Holly, and Luka met up with the family for a late lunch at the local soda fountain. The afternoon drifted sweetly into the night, and after sending Crissy and Keith home, the adults went to the oldest bar in Wyoming, for drinks and dancing. There, an old timer kept them spellbound weaving stories of the real old West, the way it truly had been.

The last night was the big meeting. It wasn't what Holly would have expected. There wasn't the long line of limousines parading up the mountainside. Instead, Michael had invited his closest neighbor, a retired cattle-baron, Walt, a multi-millionaire. Another, a local novelist named Stephen, known worldwide. Another man was an actor named Harrison, a top box office draw. Part of the diverse group was an older man named Gerry, a world-renowned lawyer. All who'd moved to Wyoming for anonymity after amassing their fortunes.

Holly leaned against the wall because Luka closed the door to the study, leaving her with the women and children. She was unhappy, to say the least. Didn't Luka trust her more than this? It was a strong indictment. There were more limits to her relationship with Luka, and they were placed where he decided she didn't belong.

She sipped hot chocolate and leisurely passed the closed

door when she found herself dawdling, leaning her ear closer to the door. She overheard an incredible conversation.

Luka's voice was shouting out.

"It's been hard keeping this secret. I've begun proceedings to file for divorce. Meaning, I need all the cash I can lay my hands on, mates. The less she knows about my holdings, the better. I have an old company and the ownership buried under paperwork. It will never be traced to me. I can imagine what the missus would say if someone told her I was buying more shares of CMT to gain control."

There was hearty laughing rumbling throughout the room.

"I need to find out who the secret buyer is to lure him out and make an offer that will force a sale to me. Then I'll be the sole owner and have all of CMT's stock."

"I'm sorry you didn't buy more shares when I offered them. The other buyer insisted on a non-disclosure clause that I signed," Michael explained anticipating Luka's disapproval.

"I understand the business, Michael. Doesn't mean I have to bloody well like it," Luka said in a tone laced with disgust.

Then the conversation drifted. One of the men asked.

"How do you like to be in a harness? You were so used to traveling?"

"Not as bad as imagined. L.A. is a brilliant location to work. I demanded no office. Give me a mobile and a convertible to work out of, and I'll call that my office."

He laughed. "It's harder on Michael. Each time I show up, he acts as if the governor's arrived. You have to relax Michael. You are COO, and CMT is your baby and needs you."

Luka is trying to buy the controlling stock in CMT.

Catherine was right. Somehow, she would keep her secret for the time being, hoping he would get comfortable and safe enough to share the news with her. But what if he never did? This was why he had so much clout at CMT. It was his company. Suddenly Kaine crept into her thoughts. Would Kaine be surprised to learn this piece of news, then again, probably not as surprised as she was?

Clearly, she'd seriously underestimated Luka Hunter. What other secrets did he have? How many more would he keep a secret?

Holly sipped her hot chocolate, captivated by the globally sophisticated and successful men, swapping their business war stories of climbing to the top of their respected fields. Even more impressive, Luka held his own.

Working close to him meant he'd brought her up-to-date on his various enterprises. But to discover these behind-the-scenes deliberations, she wondered what his reasoning was to keep the negotiations a secret from her?

Yes, Luka was an impossibly accomplished businessman at his tender age of thirty-five. She would have never guessed his mounting wealth, or power, that day he rescued her in Chelsea.

A smile curled at the corners of her lips, remembering his casual outfit, a leather bomber jacket, and tan Dockers. He was someone to reckon with — a world-class executive and the top man in the music industry.

His endless knowledge fascinated her. How fluently he spoke of the stock market, and understood the international market money exchange. His familiarity with global business deals boggled her mind. And comparing this room full of international entrepreneurs, to the more prominent clients that the firm represented, she was hard pressed to find an equally successful man at his age. Except for one, Kaine, Mr. half-billion-dollar Walker.

Holly laughed under her breath, at how she'd fallen into this vat of wealthy men. It was then she realized, other than her ritualistic check-in with Kaine each morning in the bathroom, Kaine hadn't crossed her mind until a few moments ago. It was difficult to understand exactly why. And the guilt softly caressed her conscience.

Yes, it was a good sign, because there was only one other man in the world that could make her forget Kaine Walker, and he sat on the other side of the door. She hoped Kaine's memory would develop into a worn and faded memorial of lost hopes and dreams.

In the meantime, she looked forward to a bright and happy future with Luka, the perfect holiday companion. He was there to warm her with bear hugs and hold her cold hands. He always wore his white sheepskin jacket, and underneath an assortment of soft cashmere sweaters, and a variety of Levi's with his fleecy snow boots.

When they'd visited the nearby Trout Farm and strolled out to the edge of the woods, he'd worn his old rough out boots. There was nothing pretentious about Luka Hunter.

She'd laughed with Luka, losing a snowball fight against Keith and Crissy. Then later the snow angel, he'd made, and what a snow angel he was when he stood up with snowflakes crowning his beautiful head.

He'd flashed his magnificent smile and his bright blue eyes sparkled, telling her how much he enjoyed being with her.

He must have been an incredibly lonely man before he met her. And her heart strings pull hard toward Luka Hunter.

Luka was there to snuggle close to on the couch, with his feet covered with thick red socks and his big toe boring a gaping hole in the tip. She smiled again remembering him cuddling with her, his arms wrapped tightly around her in front of the fireplace after the others slipped off to bed, giving them time alone. His brief kisses warmed her, opening her heart in a quiet way. She'd sipped hot chocolate with him, gazed into his incredible blue eyes to-die-for, wondering how this ever happened.

She'd learned a lot about him and herself. Luka, always therapeutic for her ailments, mended her broken heart until she barely noticed the jagged seam. Most nights he quickly kissed her good night at her door. No long, knee bending, fiery kisses. Never made any overtures or insinuated any pressure to enter her private chamber.

Holly learned long ago not to ask and became relaxed, feeling safe and secure with Luka. She trusted him, and she made do with watching the sparkle grow brighter in his eyes each hour they spent together. He was peaceful, easy, and comfortable to be near, especially, to snuggle up to, and keep the chill away.

Holly decided to take her hot chocolate upstairs. She had a lot to consider because Luka wanted her in a way she didn't understand repeating that he wanted to nurture their relationship the right way.

Luka Hunter was a powerful man, in charge of the most powerful music medium of her time. CMT could make or break any act simply by limiting or increasing the number of rotations allowed. And at the helm, the man that made those decisions was Luka Hunter, the man in control of her future with the show.

Holly lazily stretched the next morning. She'd been too tired to deliberate much about her recent discovery concerning Luka's global entrepreneurial dealings. The few days of rest had become a wonderful holiday. Today was the day they would leave this private paradise.

Unexpectedly, her dreamy bubble exploded.

Chapter Twenty-Five

RIGHT HERE WAITING FOR YOU

Holly stood at the kitchen sink, staring at the incredible view. Of course, Luka made up a large part of it. She probably wore the starved cat look again. Luka was outside bundled up to his rosy nose in his sheepskin coat. He'd plopped Michael's silly red knit cap on his head, then repaired the Thanksgiving snowman with Crissy as Catherine approached her.

"Holly, what I'm going to ask is none of my business. But we have developed a close friendship these past few days. I don't know if you are aware, but our bath suite is located beneath your bathroom."

"Oh, Catherine, I hope I haven't disturbed you and Michael!" Holly was mortified she'd brought a moment's discomfort to her kind-hearted host and hostess.

"It's not what you're assuming. You've been a delight to have here, and you are welcome in our home, here or in L.A., anytime. But what concerns me is what happens in the bathroom each morning. And as a mother twice removed, I recognized what I'm hearing." Catherine placed her warm, smooth hand over Holly's sympathetically.

Holly couldn't decide how to respond. The silence hit her with the realities of her situation.

"You're pregnant, aren't you?"

Holly didn't have much time left to hide her growing belly, but to her surprise, Catherine added.

"When will you and Luka announce your wonderful news?"

It had started.

Holly spent too much time with Luka. Everything was as he predicted, everyone would be sure to believe she carried Luka's heir. This would certainly be ludicrous when a carbon copy of Kaine, with dark hair and brooding blue eyes, arrived late next spring. There was no doubt she was carrying a son, a strong, handsome son like his father.

Thoughts of Kaine flooded her swiftly and unmercifully. They surrounded her memories squeezing conflicting feelings from her. She needed to forget them, memories like his gentle touch and strong, loving arms — Kaine. But arrangements needed to be made. Luka, as usual, had drawn her attention to that earlier.

This situation has an expiration date on it.

It was only a matter of time before Catherine told Michael if they hadn't discussed it already. After all, Michael signed her to do six shows for HHW, with an option to extend. How would her pregnancy affect her show?

She'd come to depend on Luka. Therefore, she hadn't made a plan, sure Luka that would. He'd troubleshoot the problem, and when he was the controlling stock owner, he could do anything he damn well wanted to her.

The force of the realization made her knees weak and almost knocked her down where she stood. Luka Hunter would not only be her boss, but he would own her show!

"Holly, I'm sorry. I didn't mean to pry. Sit here in this chair. You've lost all of your color."

Catherine quickly produced a mineral water, and Holly took a long drink. Luka owned her show for six episodes, possibly more if she resigned. Had he planned to tie her up in contracts to guarantee their future together for many years to come? This would seriously damage any possible reconciliation with Kaine. Was this what Luka planned? No, she couldn't accept that Luka was this cunning. He was more of an astute businessman.

Catherine was looking at Holly with a serious expression plaster to her face. Her compassionate eyes said they wouldn't ask any more about the pregnancy.

Holly faced Catherine. She looked her straight in the eyes, hoping to hide the escalating fear growing inside her and confessed.

"Yes, I'm pregnant. No, Luka and I have no immediate plans to announce anything."

The lie of omission was true. But she hated to deceive Catherine on such a technicality. She'd been amazingly kind and sensitive to her. How complex things were becoming again.

Reality crashed in harshly as the holiday merry-makers descended the long winding road from Freedom Mountain. Yes, even high in the Big Horn Mountains, news of

Hurrikaine and Kaine's virus made the news on the local rock station out of Casper.

"Now That I've Found You," followed on the heels of the broadcast and Michael turned it up louder as if he assumed everyone would be as happy to listen. CMT had another mega hit and airplay equaled viewers and money to Michael.

Holly wasn't happy.

She sat staring into Kaine's brooding blue eyes in the mirror of her memory. She remembered beautiful images of him singing his heart out to her at Friar Manor, and of better times in the castle.

Holly suddenly sensed Kaine near her, running his smooth hand gently over her face as if caressing expensive fur.

She listened to Kaine softly singing his love for her into her hair backstage at Friar Manor.

Never free of the man named Kaine.

Four weeks ….Kaine.

TO BE CONTINUED...

Dear Reader,

Ready to purchase **SURRENDER**, part 2, in the Hollywood series? Please take a moment and leave a few comments about your favorite scenes wherever you purchased **BLOOD**. It is crucial to the series to have immediate feedback while the pleasure from the story is fresh in your mind. Thank you for your valuable support. YOU ROCK!

One man's name on her lips…

Holly Hill's been liberated from a from a tabloid headline to becoming a celebrity with her own rock music interview show on Cable Music Television (CMT). She spends her time with the beautiful and sexy, Luka Hunter, who is always making plans for a bright future.

Another man's name in her heart…

However, memories of Kaine Walker, rock star, continue to haunt Holly. They are fighting their way to the forefront of her tormented and confused heart. She dreams of the moment she can follow her heart and walk away from Luka. But will Luka ever allow her to leave him?

Evil is a powerful aphrodisiac…

Will she resist?

Find out in SURRENDER Part 2~Hollywood

http://www.kewtownsend.com/

KEW TOWNSEND

Affairs of the Heart ~ Hollywood

SURRENDER (Part 2), *LIASION* (Part 3), *DECEPTION* (Part 4)

Affairs of the Heart Series ~ London

HEART (Part 1), *TEMPTATION* (Part 2)
PROMISES (Part 3), *DEVOTED* (Part 4), *BETRAYAL* (Part 5)

Ms. Townsend is a widow with a wonderful daughter, educator, travel and movie buff, and writes romantic music fiction set in the 1960s-1980s rock scene in the *Affairs of the Heart Series*. She lives in sunny Southern California and loves to read under a palm tree with wave's crashing along the shoreline.

KEW's love of rock music began at a young age when she returned glass Coke bottles for change to buy 45 rpm records. Her interest moved from the music to the musicians, and living in Hollywood, interviewed the Beatles when they landed at Los Angeles International Airport. Acquiring a taste for the funny Englishmen, she began dating one of the Rolling Stones that exposed her to sex, drugs, and rock and roll. Later her memories surfaced in the *Affairs of the Heart Series* where she weaves her behind the scenes anecdotes with her long love of castles, mysteries, lightning, and thunder into a romantic suspense story. Her master's degree in Cultural Anthropology and Archaeology adds to her world travels, and flavor to her novels.

CONTACT KEW

kewtownsend.com

Leave a message, a review, and sign up for the NEWSLETTER. Be first to hear about new releases, preorders, sales, prizes, giveaways, and fun events.